"WHY ARE YOU TAKING OFF YOUR CLOTHES?" L.C. DEMANDED.

"Jacket. I've only removed my jacket," Drex pointed out. He sat on the sofa and patted the cushion next to him. "Won't you join me?"

"I have to study," L.C. replied quickly.

"Are you always this argumentative?" Drex asked. "Is there something about me that naturally sets you on edge? One minute you're very human, the next you're the original ice maiden."

L.C. winced at his words. "Is that how you see me?" she asked quietly.

"Not always. When I kiss you, you respond like the warm woman I think you are. But the moment I let you go, you become distant again."

"That's because I—I really don't know you very well."

Drex slowly shook his head. "That's not even a passable excuse, Laurin Catherine. Why don't you try again."

CANDLELIGHT ECSTASY ROMANCES®

MYSTERY LADY

Eleanor Woods

Published by
Dell Publishing Co., Inc.
1 Dag Hammarskjold Plaza
New York, New York 10017

ISBN: 0-440-15997-0

Printed in the United States of America

First printing—February 1986

To Our Readers:

We have been delighted with your enthusiastic response to Candlelight Ecstasy Romances®, and we thank you for the interest you have shown in this exciting series.

In the upcoming months we will continue to present the distinctive sensuous love stories you have come to expect only from Ecstasy. We look forward to bringing you many more books from your favorite authors and also the very finest work from new authors of contemporary romantic fiction.

As always, we are striving to present the unique, absorbing love stories that you enjoy most—books that are more than ordinary romance. Your suggestions and comments are always welcome. Please write to us at the address below.

Sincerely,

The Editors
Candlelight Romances
1 Dag Hammarskjold Plaza
New York, New York 10017

CHAPTER ONE

To anyone with the time or inclination to study faces, it would have been patently clear that the smile plastered on the face of the petite, attractive cocktail waitress with dark, shoulder-length hair was forced. They had only to look into her eyes to see that her present surroundings were about as conducive to her peace of mind as running barefoot through a brier patch. They were dark green eyes with the faintest upward slant at the outer edges, and were fringed by thick sooty lashes. Not that there was any overt disapproval revealed in her movements or in the manner in which she served the patrons in her station; there wasn't. After six months of sidestepping wandering hands and being propositioned with an uncanny variety of suggestions, L. C. Carlyle had learned to cope— almost.

The job paid well, thus enabling her to retain her expression of bland disinterest, and to disregard the less than chivalrous remarks from the male members of Nikko's mixed clientele. Most of the customers were in the middle-to-upper-income bracket, usually well mannered and courteous. And she could usually handle the remarks and the off-color jokes.

But the "gentleman" presently holding her attention, one of a party of six celebrating the beginning of the New Orleans carnival season, was straining every ounce of L.C.'s patience as she tried to take his order.

She'd already sidestepped the attempted groping of her derriere by his not-so-subtle hand, equipped with more moves than a sidewinder, and refused, as politely as possible, an invitation to accompany him to his hotel for an evening she would never forget.

The man, a thin sheen of perspiration above his upper lip, leered knowingly at L.C., then made another lurching grab for her.

"Knock it off, Harv," the woman sitting next to him said shortly. "We've been thrown out of one place tonight already. Do you want it to happen again?" She threw L.C. an indifferent glance. "He'll have a double bourbon on the rocks."

L.C. turned and made her way to the small, lattice-enclosed area at one end of the long, curved mahogany bar where the cocktail waitresses turned in and received their orders. She thumped the round tray onto the shiny surface and thrust the order into Zack's waiting hands.

The tall bartender grinned, his white teeth

making a startling contrast with his dark skin and jet black mustache. "Problems?"

"Nothing I can't take care of with a whip and a chair," she snapped, then shrugged. "Sorry, Zack, I didn't mean to take it out on you. That idiot at table four is one of the reasons I'm looking for another job."

"If you can't handle the problem," Zack said, staring toward the table she indicated, "don't hesitate to call me."

L.C. eased one aching foot from its black spike pump and rubbed her toes against the back of her calf. The exaggerated footwear looked perfect with the abbreviated costumes consisting of short black skirt and red halter top worn by all the waitresses, but they played havoc with arches and backs.

"I can handle it, although it would be nice if I didn't have to do so this particular evening. I get the impression your uncle isn't exactly pleased with my methods of discouraging his more ardent customers."

"Oh, it isn't that." Zack laughed, his dark eyes skimming appreciatively over L.C.'s tiny, slender body. "It's the amount of dry cleaning he's been forced to pay for since you've been with us."

"I wonder," L.C. mused as she slipped back into her shoe and added napkins and a bowl of pretzels to her tray, "if he would prefer paying for a few fractured skulls instead?" There was a certain pleased expression on her face as she looked at Zack inquiringly.

11

"Please!" He grimaced. "I doubt even *I* could pacify him then. Maybe this kind of job isn't your cup of tea."

"You've hit on the very thing I've been telling myself lately," L.C. agreed. "That's why I've started looking around for something else. Common sense tells me that your uncle isn't likely to keep me around with my track record, and for some reason I don't seem to have the finesse required for this particular type of employment."

"Have you found anything promising?" Zack asked. He liked L.C., and he hated to see her get sacked. But his uncle was adamant that she either learn to ignore the occasional wandering hand or find something else to do. In Zack's opinion, however, L.C. would never be a success as a cocktail waitress. Her looks and her figure were enough to get any man excited. Add a few drinks, Zack sighed thoughtfully, and one had the makings of a perfect explosion—with Uncle Nikko's customer getting blasted.

"I'm going to see about two typing jobs soon," she told him. "I hate to be stuck with a headphone sounding in my ear all day, but a job's a job. With my schedule, I'm lucky to find anything."

"But just think," Zack offered encouragingly, "only two more years and you'll be able to hang out your shingle."

"If I pass the bar exam," L.C. grinned.

"Think positively," Zack said sternly. "A pessimist never gets anywhere."

"Aye, aye, sir." L.C. sketched a catchy salute and picked up the now loaded tray. She beamed sweetly up at him. "May I please think positively about the charming gentleman over there," nodding toward the loud group in the corner, "who has tried every way possible to get his hands on my behind? I would like to think 'positively' about hurting him. Perhaps a broken wrist? My heel smashing through his instep? How about a club meeting the granite thickness of his obnoxious head?"

Zack exhaled noisily and watched her walk away. He sent up a silent prayer that Uncle Nikko wouldn't put in an appearance until later . . . much later. Unfortunately, the gods turned a deaf ear to his prayer. In a sequence of events that he later remembered as one of the funniest sights he'd ever seen—but at the time wasn't funny at all—Zack saw L.C.'s body swerve to avoid the outstretched hand of the Mardi Gras reveler. He saw the man start to rise to his feet and lunge toward L.C., the fingers of his right hand aiming for the seductive bodice of the halter top.

At that precise moment it was as though each of Zack's eyes had developed a mind of its own. One saw the portly figure of his uncle standing in the doorway of the small, luxurious office off the lounge, his face full of pleasure at the sight of a full house. Zack's other

13

eye saw a tiny figure in red and black dump six drinks, a stack of napkins, and a bowl of pretzels over the head of the customer at table four.

In a flash Zack was out from behind the bar, heading toward the disturbance. Uncle Nikko, his expression thunderous, was rushing forward like a short, plump rooster. L.C. banged the tray in the center of the small table, calmly turned on her high heel and, amid the amused grins of several customers who had witnessed the outrageous behavior of the customer and L.C.'s solution to the problem, began making her way to the employees' lounge.

As she drew alongside Uncle Nikko, she favored him with a brittle smile and continued on her way. Her glance to Zack was more in the form of a resigned apology. The least said at the moment, the better, she told herself on entering the lounge.

Without pausing to consider what she'd done, L.C. began taking off the black and red uniform, replacing it with the jeans and yellow baggy sweatshirt she'd worn to the club. The black high heels were exchanged for a pair of gray suede ankle boots.

She took a navy windbreaker from a hanger and picked up her large, serviceable shoulder bag. So much for her career as a cocktail waitress, L.C. thought philosophically. Though the job had paid better than any she'd had in quite a while, she was forced to admit that fending off wandering hands and ignoring insulting remarks three evenings a week was not for her.

Just as she opened the door of the lounge and stepped into the narrow corridor, she came face to face with Uncle Nikko, Zack close on his heels. The short, portly gentleman of Greek extraction ran a quick, assessing glance over L.C.'s body.

"Are you all right?" he asked courteously.

L.C. nodded ruefully. "Yes," she said. "Thank you for asking. I'm sorry for causing you so much trouble, Mr. Constantine, but when I tell a man no, I mean just that."

"It's not your no that I find fault with, L.C.," the elderly Greek said resignedly. "It's your methods of enforcing what you say." For a moment there was a gleam of amusement in his eyes.

L.C. glanced over his shoulder at Zack, who smiled broadly, thankful that his uncle was behaving in a calmer manner than he'd expected. L.C. looked back at her former boss. "I've left my tips for this evening on the table in the lounge. If I have any money coming, I'd feel better if you would keep it to help defray the expense I'm sure I caused you."

"That won't be necessary," Nikko said sternly. "A check, including your tips for this evening, will be mailed to you tomorrow." He bowed his head slightly in her direction, then turned and walked away.

15

L.C. grinned at Zack. "Well, at least he wasn't ready to hang me."

"That's because several other customers were quick to tell him how obnoxious your inebriated swain was. You know Uncle Nikko." He grinned. "The customer comes first. So after hearing all the evidence, he bowed to the wishes of the masses—as he saw them—and asked the gentleman to leave. I don't think he was going to fire you, but when he saw you dressed to go, he was probably relieved."

"That's life," L.C. said. She thoughtfully pursed her lips, patted Zack on the arm, and stepped around him. "Thanks for everything, Zack," she said, ignoring his hand that reached out to detain her and the dark, intense glow showing in his eyes. There was no place in her life for Zack or any other man. She went out and hurried to the parking lot.

L.C. edged her decrepit twelve-year-old Chevy into the line of late-night traffic, as comfortable with the peculiar-sounding knocks and pings coming from the engine as she would have been with the precisioned purr of a Mercedes. That the vehicle was old and ugly mattered little to L.C. It was hers, and more importantly, it was paid for. Those two factors more than made up for any short-comings the car might have.

Plans for a new car and other luxury items had been placed on the back burner. But, L.C. told herself, she really didn't mind. In all probability, she reasoned, she would never be in the Mercedes income bracket. Especially if she maintained her present goal of practicing law when she passed the bar. She'd seen and read enough to realize that a domestic relations practice—with special emphasis on battered wives—wouldn't be the most lucrative field she could choose. But it would certainly be her foremost commitment. Common sense told her she would have to include personal injury and product liability cases in her practice if she wanted such mundane things in her life as food, shelter, and clothing.

Her green eyes glowed with determination as she reflected on her own experiences. She had had a husband who lacked feeling or understanding, but she'd been one of the lucky ones. There had been no children to consider when they had filed for divorce. In fact, L.C. grimly reminded herself, her particular marriage was hardly a landmark case when it came to battered wives.

Charles had been too shrewd for that, she remembered painfully. His abuse hadn't been physical. But L.C. had often wondered during the twelve months of her marriage if physical abuse was any less painful than emotional abuse. Bruises and abrasions healed, but the mind was complicated. Mean, ugly words spoken with deliberate and calculated intent left scars that only time and dedicated determination could heal. Charles had proved to be an expert at hurting people, and in the year and

17

a half since their divorce L.C. had been struggling to regain a small sense of balance in her life.

Strangely enough, she mused, it was her sense of humor, which had been such a vital facet of her personality before her marriage, that was the first familiar emotion to surface. She'd always heard that necessity was the mother of invention. In her case laughing at herself had been a definite necessity; she'd already cried a river of tears.

As L.C. stood before the door of the apartment she shared with Leslie Cambridge, she could hear faint sounds coming from the TV. Good. Leslie had a way of minimizing the ups and downs in life that left L.C. feeling better about herself.

"Good heavens!" Leslie exclaimed when L.C. closed the door behind her. "It can't be after midnight already."

"Of course it is," L.C. replied with a straight face. "Doing that needlepoint has addled your brain, Les." She walked over and dropped down onto the sofa, then leaned over and peered at the piece of work the redhead put aside. "Hmm. Does this mean we'll be seeing less of the handsome Robert?"

During the year and a half they'd been sharing an apartment, L.C. had become aware of the routine Leslie established with the various men in her life. When everything was going well, her roommate was out almost every evening. When she tired of a particular

18

man, out would come the needlepoint until another prospect arrived on the scene.

"Robert is a wimp. I simply can't believe I endured his pettiness for as long as I did," Leslie remarked acidly. She popped her reading glasses back in place and looked at her watch, then eyed L.C. with a grin. "What's your excuse? According to my watch, it's only ten fifteen. Did Uncle Nikko finally fire you?"

"Certainly not," L.C. said with feigned haughtiness. "I quit." She leaned her head back against the sofa. "Before he could fire me."

"Good for you. Did you have another unpleasant encounter with one of your customers?"

She said the words "unpleasant encounter" in a way that brought a smile to L.C.'s face. Leslie had a way of expressing herself that was amusing.

"Mmm. But I got even. He almost drowned after six drinks dropped over his repulsive head."

"How nice."

"What was Robert's problem?"

"An overactive libido that he decided was my place to correct."

"And of course you disagreed."

"Precisely. I refuse to be used by anyone."

"If he had used more finesse would you have agreed?"

"Who knows?" Leslie shrugged. "He didn't,

19

I didn't—it's a moot point. What are your plans for another job? Any likely prospects?"

"Two typing positions. One for a medical records clerk in a four-doctor clinic, the other in a prestigious law firm."

"How do you know it's prestigious?"

"I don't." L.C. grinned. "That's what the woman at the employment agency told me. Part of her sales pitch is to make each available position sound as attractive as sin. I plan to check out both jobs the day after tomorrow."

Leslie tipped her head thoughtfully to one side. "Two jobs and law school is a heavy load. Are you sure you can continue to handle it? You know—"

"I can, and I will," L.C. interrupted. "Your offer to help is appreciated, but this is something I have to do on my own. Besides, getting that student loan removed a great deal of the pressure. Now all I have to do is concentrate on keeping myself fed and clothed with a roof over my head."

"If you say so. By the way, guess who I ran into today."

"From the tone of your voice, it had to be Charles."

"Right." Leslie grimaced, her blue eyes flashing. "I bumped into him as he was coming out of Mr. B's. His companion, a dopey-looking brunette, who looked and acted as if she had more cleavage than brains, was hanging onto his arm like a limpet. He even had the gall to ask about you."

"I hope you told him that I was carrying on with at least three men and that I was never home in the evenings."

"Is that what you really want him to think?" Leslie asked curiously.

"Yes. No." She plucked at an imaginary speck on the sleeve of her shirt. "That doesn't make any sense, does it? All I know is that I don't want him to think my life is shattered just because he did everything he could during our marriage to make me believe I was a cold, frigid woman."

"Put Charles Bramlett out of your mind," Leslie scolded. "You should know by now that any man who could coolly inform his wife that he's leaving her while she's in the hospital recovering from a miscarriage leaves a great deal to be desired."

"I know all that," L.C. said stubbornly. "I know he's lower than a snake, that he has a twisted mind, and that he's cruel—now. But during the time when I thought I was in love with him and was most vulnerable, the things he said to me hurt. By the time we parted, my self-esteem was in the gutter."

"Being bitter isn't the answer," Leslie quietly reminded her. "You've done a lot to get yourself back together, but the only way you're ever going to see yourself as a very attractive and warm woman is to find time in your busy schedule for some semblance of a

21

social life." Leslie glanced resignedly at her friend. "Remember social life? You go out with men. You dress with care." Her assessing gaze ran disapprovingly over L.C.'s jeans and sweatshirt. "Which includes makeup and attractive hairdos."

L.C. laughed in spite of herself. "Are you implying that I'm a frump?"

"Not at all. The Greek would never have hired you if you'd been unattractive. All I'm trying to do is make you really look at yourself. With the right makeup and clothes you could be a knockout. You could dazzle any man you choose."

"Dazzling them isn't exactly what I have in mind," L.C. muttered grimly. "I'd much prefer inflicting pain."

"Don't be ridiculous," Leslie retorted. "You can't go around forever hating all men simply because you picked the scuzz of the year for a husband."

"You make me sound paranoid."

"You are. But there's hope for you. What you need is to meet a real rake."

"Why a rake?" L.C. asked, puzzled.

"Because a woman knows from the beginning that he isn't sincere. With that premise in mind, what follows can be enjoyable for both people involved. Believe me, L.C., a relationship like that can do wonders for one's morale."

"Do you have anyone in mind?" L.C. asked dryly. Really, she thought irritably, there were moments when she entertained serious doubts regarding her roommate's intelligence. Leslie knew all the details of L.C.'s disastrous marriage. They had been friends since college, so when Charles did his vanishing act, Leslie brought L.C. home to the apartment they now shared. Yet here she was, yammering away about men and how they could put everything right in L.C.'s life.

"Not really." Leslie shook her head, ignoring the less than pleasant glare being directed toward her. "However, since it is the carnival season, it wouldn't hurt at all for you to go to some of the parties. We've gotten a lot of invitations, you know. I'm not suggesting that you jump into bed with the first man you see, L.C." She sighed resignedly. "But it stands to reason that you can't continue your bitter vendetta with all men over the age of twelve."

"I don't have the appropriate clothes for the sort of parties and dances you're talking about."

"Then go out in the morning and buy a couple of dresses. You've got a few dollars tucked away. Spend them on yourself."

"That's for emergencies," L.C. argued.

"How aptly put," Leslie muttered. "Consider yourself the emergency, in the loosest sense of the word. At the rate you're pushing yourself, you'll also be a prime candidate for a nervous breakdown. You still have your other part-time job with the detective agency, so you aren't going to starve. For once in your life, do something wild."

L.C. regarded her roommate with an almost virulent gleam in her green eyes. "The last time I did something wild, I married Charles."

"Correction, sweetie," Leslie frowned. "That little trek down the aisle was suicidal. So plan on spending a long lunch hour tomorrow doing some shopping. You're going to a dance tomorrow night."

CHAPTER TWO

L.C. paused in the arched entryway, her gaze casually taking in the large ballroom. The theme of the occasion was "Some Enchanted Evening," and the room had been skillfully and beautifully decorated to give one an illusion of having stepped into a world of starlight and magic.

The entire area overhead had been deftly draped in a shadowy material through which hundreds of tiny twinkling lights shone like stars. By means of expert lighting a full moon cast its brilliance upon the jeweled heads of the revelers. The orchestra was located on a greenery-bedecked revolving dais in the center of the festivities. A sparkling waterfall cascaded down each side of the dais, forming a pool in the front. The colorful gowns worn by the women reminded L.C. of a beautiful, continuous rainbow.

Suddenly her gaze shifted to a tall, tanned, dark-haired man she had noticed earlier. At the moment he was escorting a dance partner back to her table.

This was the first opportunity L.C. had had to scrutinize the man, and she took full advantage of it. As her eyes roamed up and down the length of his powerfully built body, there was a curious gleam in their green depths. Though he looked perfectly at ease in the formal attire he was wearing, L.C. knew instinctively he would be equally at ease in worn denims and a comfortable shirt. There was an aura of strength about him, a special confidence that she hadn't noticed in any of the other men she'd seen during the evening. There was also a hint of cruelty in the sculptured harshness of his features in spite of the smile he was lavishing on the woman with him, a harshness that sent a peculiar shiver of apprehension racing up and down L.C.'s spine. Yet . . . when she saw him turn as he started to walk away, then pause and look toward her table, she felt an equal moment of excitement.

He was a total stranger, with a large party at a table across the room from where L.C., Leslie, their dates, and two other couples were seated. L.C. had been dancing the first dance with Vic Longino, her date, when she first became aware of someone staring at her. She turned her head to the right, the sound of Vic's voice rumbling pleasantly in her ear, and looked straight into the most startling pair of eyes she'd ever seen.

They were dark, and set beneath thick black brows. Sooty lashes fringed their coolly assessing gaze, and L.C. had felt goose bumps springing up on her skin. To her chagrin, before she had time to turn her head, she saw the corner of his mouth quiver with—was it amusement?—then watched as one brow lifted mockingly.

The next time she encountered his gaze had been when she was standing talking with several people close to the long buffet table. She'd suddenly felt compelled to look over her shoulder. When she did, it was to find the rakish stranger's gaze sweeping over her. Only this time, instead of looking away as she'd done before, L.C.'s lips were the ones to quiver with amusement—it was *her* brow that arched mockingly. After several seconds of deliberate appraisal she allowed one smooth shoulder to lift slightly, dismissively, then turned back to the conversation at hand.

Returning to the present, L.C. skirted the dance floor and made her way back to her table.

"I was about to come look for you," Leslie murmured as L.C. sat down at the table. "Is anything wrong?"

"Not a thing," L.C. answered with a broad smile. "As a matter of fact I'm having a marvelous time."

"Then what took you so long?" Leslie persisted. She was anxious for her friend to have a good time. To Leslie's way of thinking her roommate's emotional withdrawal from any sort of social life had gone on long enough.

27

Charles Bramlett had really done a number on L.C., but Leslie had her own methods for restoring egos and self-esteem.

"The ladies' room was unbelievably crowded," L.C. replied, then turned to Vic. "I'm sorry, what did you say?"

"I said I was afraid you had deserted me. You know, I've been hounding Leslie for months to get me a date with you," Vic told her.

"Well, I'm glad you persevered," L.C. said, "and that your cousin was successful. I'm really enjoying myself."

"Great. That means I shouldn't have too much difficulty in monopolizing all your free time for the next two weeks," he replied in a perfectly serious voice.

"Only two weeks?" L.C. feigned disappointment. "What happens after that? Do I turn into a pumpkin?"

"Oh, no." Vic grinned engagingly. "After that length of time I'm positive you won't be able to resist my irrepressible charm and handsome face."

"Ahh, modesty." L.C. laughed. "I do admire a man who's modest."

"Does that mean you'll have dinner with me tomorrow evening?"

"Dinner sounds nice, but I'm afraid I can't. I have a class from seven to ten," L.C. told him.

"That's right," Vic replied. "You're in law school, aren't you? Somehow I can't imagine

28

you in a court of law, vigorously defending some felon."

"Really? Would it help if I were several inches taller and about fifty pounds heavier?" Underneath her impish grin there was a certain resentment.

"Okay," Vic said apologetically. "I realized the moment I said it that it sounded like a sexist remark. I'm sorry. Being a woman has nothing to do with it, believe me. It's just that you're so tiny . . ." He shook his head. "Doesn't it frighten you when you consider that you'll be defending people from all walks of life? I mean"—he shrugged—"you will have some undesirables thrown in there."

"Of course I will," L.C. argued. "I can hardly expect a clientele of sterling characters, can I? As for being frightened"—she shook her head—"I can honestly say I haven't given that particular aspect of my career much thought. I suppose there'll be time enough for that, if and when it happens."

Vic gave her a comically level look. "Don't you realize you've shattered my ego by showing me that you're braver than I am?"

"Don't worry." L.C. laughed and patted his hand. "I promise not to tell another living soul."

This set off another teasing round, with Vic bemoaning the number of "men's" positions being taken over by women, while L.C. defended her sex. They were so engrossed in their argument that neither of them was aware of the tall, dark-headed man standing behind them until L.C. felt the barest touch of a hand on her shoulder. She looked up, her breath catching in her throat as she saw who it was.

"If your escort has no objections, may I have this dance?" The question was courteous, but L.C. got the distinct impression that Vic's opinion was of little consequence.

Out of consideration for his feelings, L.C. looked at Vic, although her hand had already been caught in a warm, strong grasp that sent shivers of excitement scampering up her arm. She felt herself being pulled to her feet even as Vic voiced his assent.

Once on the dance floor, and with her left hand still clasped in the strong grip, L.C. felt the warmth of an arm slipping into place against her back. She looked up—and up—until her gaze met the enigmatic eyes staring intently at her. Staring was putting it mildly. Her partner seemed to be committing each of her features to memory.

Finding herself tongue-tied with a man, or anyone else for that matter, was a new experience for L.C. For the life of her she couldn't think of a single intelligent thing to say. She'd thought him striking at a distance, but up close he was devastating. Her heart was pounding, and she was sure her palms were damp with perspiration.

"Are you a native Orleanean?" he asked,

the deep tone of his voice sounding like the feel of soft velvet against her skin.

"Actually, I was born in Florida, but I've lived here long enough to consider myself a native," she told him. "And you? Are you visiting friends here for the carnival season?" It wasn't much of an icebreaker, but she supposed it was better than an uncomfortable silence.

"My business brings me into the city often enough for me to keep an apartment here." He glanced at her left hand and the old-fashioned ring there, three diamonds in a delicate filigree setting, a gift from her mother. "Am I correct in assuming this isn't a wedding ring?"

"I'm not married, if that's what you're asking," L.C. said simply, then felt her tongue stick to the roof of her mouth again. She was dying to ask him the same question, but didn't. She also wanted to ask him what exactly his business was, but held back. Perhaps it would be best to save both questions until a little later. So far, the band had been more than generous, and each dance was rather lengthy. Inquiring about his marital status, his professional interests, along with making two or three comments regarding the weather, L.C. reasoned, should get her through the next few minutes without looking like a complete fool.

"May I share your joke?" His sensuous

31

mouth twitched with amusement and his dark eyes twinkled.

"I beg your pardon?" L.C. asked, startled.

"You were almost smiling," she was told. "In fact, you were looking enormously pleased with yourself."

L.C. did smile then, a rosy hue of embarrassment showing in her cheeks. "I'm afraid I was trying to figure out how best to space the three obvious topics of conversation—your marital status, your professional interests, and of course the weather—so that it would appear we were enjoying our conversation."

To her surprise, she heard the low rumble of a chuckle start in his chest, its sound pleasant to her ears. "Then it's appearances you're worried about, correct?"

"Of course." She grinned teasingly. "It would be embarrassing for some other man to see you looking bored. That wouldn't do a single positive thing for my reputation."

His dark brown eyes dropped to the plunging neckline of her green dress and the expanse of creamy cleavage, then slowly worked their way back up to her face. "Believe me, boredom is the farthest thing from my mind."

"Hasn't anyone ever told you that it isn't nice to stare at or draw attention to a specific part of a person's body?"

"Was I staring?" he asked with all the innocence of a fox in a henhouse.

"Drooling is more like it," she bluntly informed him.

"Ah, you'll have to forgive my rude behavior," he said with a perfectly straight face. "My eyesight is deplorable."

"So is your ability to tell a lie," L.C. said sternly, although the gleam of amusement in her eyes took the sting out of her remark. "You're staring again," she pointed out breathlessly. He was, and she found it unnerving to be the object of such dedicated scrutiny.

"It's just occurred to me that I don't know your name."

L.C. started to tell him but held back, Leslie's frivolous remark that she needed to meet a genuine rake running through her mind. She'd probably met the rake of the year, she told herself, but rakes and law school, plus holding down two part-time jobs, didn't seem to go together. One would more than likely infringe on time needed for the other, and L.C. knew she had little time to pursue a social life such as Leslie had in mind for her.

"Need I remind you of the season?" She smiled. "This is carnival time. Names aren't important during Mardi Gras—especially in New Orleans."

"A lady of mystery, hmm?" And though there were no outward signs of displeasure, L.C. could sense the annoyance in the rigidity of his arm against her back.

At that moment the band brought the music to an end, and L.C. found herself free of his touch, other than his hand at her waist as he began making way for them through the crowd to her table.

"Will you be attending any of the other carnival balls and parties?" he asked.

"If my schedule permits."

"In that case we'll most likely see each other again."

They reached the table and he was seating her by the time the rest of her party began showing up. The feel of warm hands on her shoulders and the quiet murmur of "Goodnight, mystery lady" close to her ear brought an openly curious look from Leslie, which L.C. blithely ignored.

"I know I've seen that face somewhere before," Leslie said in a raised voice for the second time since their return to the apartment. They were in their respective bedrooms, carrying on a conversation as though they were in the same room. "If only I could remember," she continued, consumed with the need to identify the man L.C. had danced with.

It was almost two thirty, and though she'd really enjoyed herself, L.C. was openly groaning at the late hour: she had to be at work at eight o'clock the next morning.

"Put it out of your mind, Les," she called back to her roommate. "Most likely we won't ever see him again." But something inside L.C. found that particular thought disturbing.

34

She didn't know his name, where he worked, or anything about him, but she definitely wanted to see him again. If for no other reason, she told herself, than that he had, in a manner of speaking, pursued her. She'd seen in his eyes the look of a man who desires a woman, and she was the woman.

"Don't be ridiculous," Leslie told her as she strolled into L.C.'s room, her face devoid of makeup. "You don't dismiss a man like that without a thought."

"Then take out an ad in the paper. 'Will the man who danced with the woman wearing a green dress without a front, at last night's carnival ball please call such and such a number.' That should get his attention," L.C. replied dryly.

"Aren't you the least bit curious?"

"Of course I am, but not to the extent that I want to spend the remainder of the night hashing and rehashing each second I was with him. I have to go to work in the morning, and I have that interview at the law firm."

"Well, I have to work too," Leslie reminded her.

"Sure you do." L.C. smiled sweetly, though the smile never quite reached her eyes. "But your boss is away, and there's a very capable receptionist who will answer the phone for you. If you're an hour or so late nothing will be said."

Leslie lifted her shoulders in a gesture of amused helplessness and smiled. "I happen to have a pussycat for a boss. What more can I say?"

"Good night would be great for starters. You might follow that by going to bed." L.C. glared at her.

"You have absolutely no tact." Leslie chuckled as she turned and walked unconcernedly from the room.

But tact was the farthest thing from L.C.'s mind as she turned off the lamp and slipped into bed. Her mind and thoughts were saturated with pictures of a tall, tanned, dark-haired man with eyes like black crystal pools. Even the scent of him still lingered with her. It was distinctive, like a fall day after a brief shower—clean and brisk.

When sleep overtook her, she dreamed of dancing in the arms of the stranger. They laughed together, his eyes adoring her, never leaving her face.

"The results of your typing test are fantastic," the tall brunette said as she hurried back into the room and took her seat behind the desk. She reached for L.C.'s employment application, her lips thoughtfully pursed as she looked it over. "I see that you're also working part-time at Lamoyne Detective Agency. Is there any chance of your giving up that position in order to work for us exclusively?"

"I'm afraid not," L.C. said. "Part-time positions aren't that easy to find, and Louis Lamoyne has gone out of his way to accommodate my schedule. Another reason I wouldn't consider leaving him at this particular time is that the full-time secretary in his office is pregnant."

"Oh, well, if you won't change your mind, we'll have to make do with whatever time you can give us. As I'm sure the woman at the employment agency told you, we have several part-time employees in the typing pool. A law firm this size has a mountain of paperwork. Can you start tomorrow afternoon?"

"Tomorrow will be fine." L.C. stood, looking brisk and professional in the moss-green shirtwaist, the wide paisley belt accentuating her tiny waist. "Should I check in with you when I get here or find my own way to the typing pool?"

"Stop by here, please." Brenda Foley flashed her friendly smile again. "It's not that difficult to find, but with the layout of the building it can be confusing. Besides, it will give us a chance to get to know each other better. I must say, I admire you tremendously for taking on the load you have. Law school and two jobs must get pretty hectic."

"Believe me it does," L.C. agreed. "I suppose the only saving grace about the entire situation is that I'm so busy I don't have time to think about the hectic pace." She turned toward the door. "Thank you for seeing me, Miss Foley, and—"

"Brenda, please."

"Brenda. I'll be here at one thirty tomorrow. See you then."

As L.C. rounded the corner of the last corridor leading to the elevator, two men emerged from the door of an office she'd just passed. The taller of the two, who was pointing to a particular section on a certain page of the opened file he had in his hand, happened to glance up just as the elevator opened and L.C. stepped in.

For a split second Drex Halloran stood like a statue, staring disbelievingly at his mystery lady. His surprise was replaced by a sudden rush of movement as he thrust the file into the hands of the startled young man with whom he'd been talking and sprinted toward the elevator. Unfortunately, before he'd taken more than four or five long strides, he saw the heavy doors close with a swoosh.

He stood motionless, a scowl of annoyance descending over his craggy features. There was no doubt about it, he told himself; that was the woman he'd danced with the night before.

He'd spent the greater part of the evening watching her. He knew the way she unconsciously tilted her head to one side as she talked, and the seductive curtain of coal black hair that brushed the curve of her cheekbones. Her walk was proud, her head held regally—like a tiny queen.

It was his mystery lady all right. His gaze became shuttered as he pondered the situation. But what was she doing here? Was she a client? He rubbed his chin with a large hand. His firm specialized in personal injury cases. Could she be involved in one of those? Whatever the reason, someone would have to have seen her.

He suddenly turned around and strode toward the large reception area, a pleased expression on his face. In his mind he was already deciding on the type of flowers he would send her. Something old-fashioned, like sweetheart roses or violets, maybe daisies. Drex had a feeling his mystery lady didn't give two hoots for long-stemmed roses.

"Let me have a look at your appointment book, Caroline," he told the receptionist when he reached her desk. "Do you remember seeing a small brunette wearing a green dress within the last hour or so?" he asked as he scanned the page.

"Sorry, Mr. Halloran. I took a long lunch hour today in the dentist's chair." She pointed to her right jaw, which had a puffy appearance.

"I'm sorry," Drex muttered sympathetically. "If you need to take some time off, please feel free to do so. Who filled in here while you were out?"

"Probably one of the temps from the typing pool. What with two secretaries out on vacation, it's rather hectic getting someone to cover. Is something wrong, Mr. Halloran? Did I miss someone important?"

"No, Caroline," Drex assured her. "You haven't made any kind of a mistake. I was just curious about something." He flashed her a smile that left the impressionable receptionist with a giddy feeling in spite of her aching jaw. "Take care of that tooth," he threw over his shoulder as he turned and disappeared into another office.

"Some weird person by the name of Vladimir called to tell you that your night class has been canceled," Leslie yelled from her bedroom the moment L.C. entered the apartment. "Vic also called, and when he found you were free for the evening he wanted to know if you'd like to go with him to the dance tonight."

L.C.'s response was a groan of relief at the first message and a grimace at the second. She dropped to an inelegant sprawl on the sofa and closed her eyes. She was exhausted.

"Did you hear me?" Leslie demanded as she padded into the living room, her hair wrapped in a towel and grayish goop covering her face.

L.C. opened her eyes and stared at the apparition standing over her. "Jeez!" she exclaimed. "You look like a freaked-out mummy."

"Never mind how I look." Leslie pushed her roommate's legs aside and sat down. "Did you hear what I said about the night class?"

"I heard."

"And Vic? Are you interested in going to the dance?"

"Don't you and your cousin ever get tired of partying?" L.C. asked against the yawn that threatened to split her face.

"For heaven's sake, L.C. This is the carnival season."

"So? Doesn't the body get tired during carnival season the same as it does any other time of the year?"

"You're being deliberately obtuse." Leslie frowned. "It's tradition. And just for the record, sweetie, I can remember a time when you thought nothing of dancing all night and working all day."

"That was B.C."

"I beg your pardon?"

"You know, like B.C. and A.D. I think of my life in terms of before Charles and after Charles."

"You are sick," Leslie told her. "And I refuse to allow you to wallow in self-pity. Call Vic and tell him you'll go with us."

"I really am tired," L.C. argued. She knew the dance would do her worlds of good, but two nights in a row were a bit much. "Remember, you keep up this hectic social pace all year long. I've only just begun to reestablish myself, and it takes some getting used to."

"Nonsense. If I don't push you, you'll spend all your free time right here on this sofa. Besides, what nicer man could you be with than Vic? I know he's not your type. In fact"—she

41

frowned—"I'm not exactly certain whose type he is. But at least he's nice."

"What manner of bribe did you dangle before him to get him to ask me out?" L.C. grinned. "In case you've forgotten, I've known him for nearly three years without his showing the slightest interest in me. Now he's acting as though I'm the answer to his prayers."

"Have you forgotten you were married when you met him?" Leslie reminded her. "Also, since your divorce, you haven't been exactly chomping at the bit for male companionship."

"Well, regardless of the reason, I think Vic is nice, and he's fun to be with. He's not nearly as pushy as his cousin."

Leslie took the dig without the slightest show of its having wounded her. "So at this stage in your life what more could you want?"

What more indeed? L.C. wondered some time later as she soaked in a warm bath. She'd pacified Leslie by calling Vic and accepting his invitation. While she was going along with the plans that seem to have been made for her, though, she was thinking about a tall, dark-haired man with deep brown eyes. Was he also a devotee of the carnival cult? Would he be present at the dance later in the evening?

And what if he is? she asked herself. What will it mean to you if he's present? More than likely he'll have a date. The most you'll see of him will be at a distance while he enjoys the evening with another woman. It's highly improbable that he'll pursue you with such dedication the second time. Look upon dancing with him last night as an added moment of excitement to the evening. Excitement—regardless of how small an amount—is something that's been missing from your life for some time now. So don't let the few minutes you were in his arms ruin your chances of having a good time tonight. Like Leslie said, Vic is nice, and he's safe. Enjoy being with him, and stop chasing rainbows.

And yet, she thought honestly, there was some deep-seated desire in her to find more in a man than just the kind, easy friendship she knew Vic would offer. She wanted to see passion in a man's eyes when he looked at her, wanted to feel the quiver of desire when he held her in his arms. Was that so terrible of her? She let her thoughts float back to the stranger of the evening before. Dare she become involved in a game of subtle seduction with him? Would she ever even see him again?

CHAPTER THREE

The moment they arrived at the grand ballroom, L.C. found her gaze unconsciously
scanning the crowd for a pair of broad shoulders and a somewhat harsh, craggy face.
When she was unsuccessful in her search, she
stifled her disappointment and threw herself
into the party spirit with a determination that
brought almost instantaneous results. Again
she and Vic had joined Leslie and her date—a
different man from the evening before—
along with two other couples. It was a conge-
nial group, and none of the women in their
party were allowed to sit out a single dance.

An element of excitement was added by
the simple masks worn by men and women
alike. Leslie had picked up one for herself and
L.C., narrow creations covered in satin and
outlined in sequins, the colors matching their
dresses.

"Where are the plumes for our hair?" L.C.
had teased her friend when the masks had
been whipped from a bag and one had been
given to her earlier at their apartment.

"What on earth are you talking about?"

"For some insane reason," L.C. had laughingly explained, "when I see masks like these, I automatically think of plumes bobbing over our heads as we cavort and frolic our way through the evening. I think it must come from seeing a picture of my mother dressed like that for some costume ball."

"See how lucky you are?" Leslie had chuckled. "All you're forced to contend with is a simple mask."

"For which I'm eternally grateful," L.C. had muttered as she tried to slip the slim side prongs of the mask into place without messing up her hair.

"Speaking of your mother, have you heard from her lately?" Leslie had asked.

"She phoned me at work last week. She still sounds madly in love with Clayton and seems really happy. She still wants me and my brother to visit them in Hawaii, so I guess that's a good omen."

"Maybe Clayton is the man she's been looking for all along."

"I sincerely hope so. After two divorces and three marriages, it's about time she found what she wants," L.C. had remarked dryly.

By the time their dates arrived, L.C. had put her mother's personal life out of her mind. The look mirrored in Vic's eyes as they swept over the salmon-colored taffeta dress was enough to make any woman feel like a million dollars, L.C. told herself.

It was midway through the evening and L.C., having readily given her consent for Vic to dance with an old friend, found her way through one of several French doors leading to a terrace that overlooked the city. She hoped to rest her aching feet and catch a breath of fresh air.

She hurried toward a round, massive column, one of several along the terrace, and leaned against it. Without caring that she was attending one of the major social events of the year, she calmly removed first one foot from its shoe and then the other. The coolness of the flagstone floor rushed through her nylons, and L.C. breathed a clearly audible "Ahh." She cushioned her head against the column and closed her eyes, quite certain she'd never felt anything as satisfying.

"Is it really that bad?" The deep voice that broke through the muted sounds of music, laughter, and voices wasn't really a surprise. In truth she'd been waiting all evening to hear its gravelly tone. Instead of pretending to be shocked, L.C. remained as she was, except for the tiny smile that appeared on her lips.

"That bad," she agreed. "I'm sure my feet will never be the same again. I thought being a cocktail waitress and having to wear spike heels was bad, but dancing nonstop for three hours is worse."

She opened her eyes and found him standing only inches in front of her, his large body propped against the waist-high railing that surrounded the terrace. The light spilling from the ballroom cast half his masked face into bold prominence, leaving the other half in shadowy darkness. He was once again dressed in a tuxedo, and he looked magnificent. Some men, when forced into formal attire, looked stiff and uncomfortable, but not this man. He looked comfortable and in total command. For some reason, that pleased her.

"I wondered if I would see you again," she said simply, then quietly questioned herself as to why it seemed so easy, so simple, to be this direct and frank with a man whose name she didn't even know.

"I was unavoidably detained," he responded in the same open manner. "Have you been waiting long?"

She was suddenly possessed with the wild, crazy sensation of wanting to tease, of wanting to be in charge of the moment with this very large, very intimidating man. The fact that he'd singled her out both evenings was as heady as a potent wine. That small victory in reality became an unbelievable triumph in her mind. She smiled. "Didn't you hear me say that after three hours of dancing my feet are worn down to the very bone?"

Drex felt something tighten in his chest, then explode with equal suddenness as he saw her smile, and watched the way her lips parted to reveal even, white teeth. He felt his mouth go dry as he stared at her, unable to fathom the inexplicable fascination that drew him to her. She certainly wasn't the most beautiful woman he'd known; she wasn't tall, nor was her figure the most curvaceous he'd seen. And damn it all, she wasn't even a good armful.

But her skin was like velvet, and when she looked at him with those green, green eyes with their sexy slant, he could feel his insides burning.

"Perhaps I can do something to make you more comfortable," Drex said, breaking the electric silence between them.

The words were barely out of his mouth when L.C. saw him bend toward her, then felt his arms behind her knees and shoulders. She was whisked from the floor and into his arms as easily as if she were a baby.

"I'll admit this is nice"—she regarded him with open skepticism from her lofty position —"but aren't you afraid we'll receive more than our share of attention?" She might be forced to change her strategy in regard to who was in charge, she thought fleetingly. While being carried in a pair of strong arms was certainly pleasant enough, it left her at a distinct disadvantage.

"I promise there won't be a single embarrassing moment," Drex murmured against the top of her head.

"That's nice," L.C. said faintly, torn between her pleasure in the hard, sinewy strength beneath her fingers as she clutched his arm and shoulder and her displeasure in not having the slightest idea where he was taking her. She heard the rumble of laughter in his chest and quickly glanced up to his face. At that precise moment she was thankful for the mask she was wearing. She hoped it would keep him from seeing how truly rattled she was.

"Frightened?" he smiled down at her, his warm gaze turning her blood to quicksilver as it scampered through her veins.

"It reoccurred to me that I don't know you at all." L.C. tried for a brave front, but got the feeling it was a wasted effort. At the moment she didn't feel brave at all. She felt intimidated.

"I think this will do," Drex said quietly, sidestepping her attempt to learn his name as smoothly as she'd handled his question on the same subject the evening before.

L.C. found herself being placed on a thickly cushioned wicker love seat. But instead of sitting down beside her, as she assumed he would do, Drex transferred one hand to the top of the seat behind her shoulders and the other one to the arm at her side.

His face was so close she could see several tiny scars along the angle of his square jaw and chin. She wondered at the small imperfections, surprised by her curiosity regarding this man. When she sensed he was about to kiss her, she tried to turn away. But a strong hand, its fingers firmly attaching themselves to her chin, put an end to that brief moment of rebellion.

She saw his lips come nearer, slowly, quietly, like a spirit on soundless feet. The first touch of his mouth against hers was light, strong, but gentle. His tongue touched and explored the delicate curve of her lips, building excitement within her as it familiarized itself with this new and interesting quest.

He made no effort to caress her with his hands, L.C. realized hazily; it was the erotic manipulations of his mouth that held her a prisoner in velvet bonds. When his tongue stormed the fiery sweetness of her mouth there wasn't the barest hint of resistance to be found. L.C. responded willingly, each nerve ending extended to its fullest capacity. She couldn't begin to define all the reasons behind her attraction for this stranger—they were too complicated—but it was there. It had lurked in the shadows of her thoughts since that first moment she'd looked around and found herself staring into his dark eyes.

She'd thought herself in love with Charles, but she could never remember this kind of urgency at any time of their lovemaking, and she wasn't sure she was ready for it now. Charles had left her feeling as limp and ugly as a dishrag. She'd promised herself that she'd never again let a man become such an integral part of her life that her self-esteem could be shattered by a few well-chosen words. The two or three men she'd dated since her divorce, even Vic . . . Oh, Lord, Vic! L.C.'s mind flipped into overdrive, reality thrusting its way past the hazy aura of seduction to which she'd become a willing victim. How could she have been so careless? She'd forgotten all about Vic.

She placed her hands against the stranger's darkly clad shoulders and pushed at the master of seduction slowly but surely drawing her into his web.

"Vic," she managed in a wobbly, cracking voice. "I have to get back to Vic."

Drex slowly raised his head, his expression incredulous. "Vic?"

"My date," she rushed to explain, praying the mask would hide her confusion. "He probably thinks I've gone off somewhere and croaked."

A large hand, its unsteadiness adding an extra boost to L.C.'s rapidly inflating ego, found its way to the curve of her cheek. "I can, and will, testify to the fact that you haven't 'croaked.' If you were any more alive, I'd be making love to you right here."

As flattering as the words were, L.C. found she resented the implication. They went a long way toward helping her regain a healthy perspective on a situation that had suddenly gone haywire. Listen, kiddo, she quietly lectured, this is a man, and not your common, ordinary garden variety. He's all M-A-N. As such, he's equally blessed with the chauvinistic reasoning that you're a ripe plum, ready to fall into his arms at the snap of his fingers. Don't fall into that trap again.

She reached out boldly and tapped him sharply on the chin. "Aren't you assuming rather a lot on one kiss?" L.C. said briskly.

"Am I?" Drex replied silkily, his eyes glittering behind the mask. "You tell me."

How could she, with him standing over her, tempting her with his touch . . . with his lips? she was of a mind to tell him. Instead, she scrambled further along the love seat, then quickly got to her feet.

"One kiss is hardly an invitation into my bed." She looked about for her shoes and finally spied them by the column where she'd first stepped out of them. Without another word to the displeased man beside her, she started forward, only to find her arm caught in a firm grip.

"Is it really this Vic character you're worried about, or are you too much of a coward to leave all this and slip away with me?"

L.C. smiled brightly, though her heart was pumping and her arm was tingling from his touch. "Vic is a very nice person, and I really do think you'd be disappointed if I were to take you up on your offer." She whirled and ran, pausing only long enough to whisk her shoes from the floor before she disappeared into the ballroom.

Drex walked over to the banister and stared into the night, his thoughts embroiled with a number of ideas and ways to find out more about his green-eyed minx. He hadn't bothered asking her name again, knowing full well she wouldn't tell him. He'd played along with her little game this evening thinking that before the night was over they'd be alone together in his apartment.

That she hadn't gone along with his plans annoyed Drex. His gaze narrowed thoughtfully as he remembered her response to his kiss. Since indifference definitely wasn't an obstacle, that meant there had to be someone else; that also rankled. Drex couldn't remember when he'd been so callously dismissed by a woman for another man. In fact he couldn't remember ever having been denied by a woman.

He raised one large square hand and adjusted his mask. If Miss Green Eyes wanted to play cagey, he would show her that two could participate in that little game. With the humorless glitter of retaliation in his eyes, he strolled back inside. There had been a tall attractive redhead at her table last night . . .

L.C. was almost gritting her teeth in frustration as she listened to Vic and Leslie going on about the old friends they'd seen at the dance, how they'd changed, who was dating whom now and who had recently divorced. She shifted restlessly in her chair in the living room of the apartment, longing to jump to her feet and tell Vic to scram so that she could put his cousin through the third degree.

Finally, when L.C. was on the verge of screaming, Leslie bade them good night and left the room.

Vic turned to L.C. "I know being out two evenings in a row is playing havoc with your studies, but if I promise to have you home early will you have dinner with me tomorrow evening?"

"I'm afraid I can't," she said firmly as she stood, determined to bring the evening to a close. "I'm starting a new job tomorrow, and as you just mentioned, I have to get in some studying."

"Then may I call you later in the week?"

"Of course," L.C. said, edging him toward the door.

At the door she stood passively as he kissed her, feeling the sum total of nothing.

Apparently this lack of response was of little consequence to Vic. He smiled down at her, caressed her cheek, and left.

The moment the door closed behind him, L.C. flew down the short hall and barged into her roommate's bedroom like a small tornado.

"What did you tell him?" she demanded the moment she came to a halt in the middle of the room.

Leslie, who was just emerging from the bath adjoining her bedroom, held a tiny white jar in one hand and was calmly smoothing its contents onto her face and neck. She gave

L.C. a bemused look. "Vic? You heard every word spoken between us."

"I'm not talking about Vic, and you damn well know it." L.C. glared at her. "I'm talking about the man that asked you to dance—and kept you on the dance floor through three numbers. The same one you were so sure you knew last night. What did the two of you talk about?"

"Well really, L.C.!" Leslie pretended to be insulted. "Don't you think you're being silly? He's a handsome man. Sexy too."

"I know all that, but I want to know what you talked about," L.C. persisted. "Did he ask you anything about me?"

"Gee!" Leslie raised her large baby blues toward the ceiling, her expression one of feigned innocence. "We talked about so many things. I really can't remember. Was there something in particular you wanted me to find out for you?"

"No!" L.C. snapped, her brow furrowed as she bore down on her friend. "I didn't want you to babble like a veritable fount of information either." She planted her small body directly in front of Leslie, her fists on her hips. "Now, talk. And don't give me all that garbage about not being able to remember."

"Dear me," the redhead chuckled. "You really are in a state, aren't you?"

"Not half the state I'm going to be in if you don't tell me what I want to know."

"Well, let me see. He was very complimentary on my dress, which I thought was a nice touch, don't you?" At L.C.'s mulish expression, Leslie thought it prudent to get on with the story. "He was curious about where I worked, what my hobbies were, and how long I'd lived in New Orleans. By the time I was convinced I'd found a suitable replacement for Robert, he completely shattered my ego by showering me with a barrage of questions about you." Leslie plucked a tissue from a box sitting on her dressing table and wiped her hands. "That's about it."

L.C. stamped one small foot in frustration. "You are without a doubt the most irritating person I've ever known! What did you tell him about me?"

"Well, let's just say that by now your mysterious suitor probably knows as much about you as your mother and your brother Ted do."

"You didn't!"

"Don't be such a goose. Of course I did." She grinned. "Naturally, I didn't go into the sordid details of your marriage, but by the time he'd finished questioning me, he was well acquainted with one L. C. Carlyle. I did think it best to leave out your places of employment."

L.C. took two steps to the right, then dropped down on the edge of the bed. "Thanks, Leslie. You've really done me a terrific favor," she remarked flatly.

"What on earth are you so worried about? He isn't married, he's pure, unadulterated male, and he's interested in you. As much as I care for my cousin Vic, there's no comparison between the two men."

"It doesn't take a genius to figure that out," L.C. muttered.

"Then what's the problem?"

"It's—I—" She lifted her hands in a helpless gesture. "I can't explain it. I only know I'm not ready for a man like . . ." Her head swung around, her eyes wide as she stared at Leslie. "Did you find out his name?"

"Drex Halloran. Even his name has a sexy ring to it, doesn't it?"

"Never mind the sexy ring, do you know him?" L.C. demanded.

"Should I?"

"Ohh." L.C. closed her eyes and shook her head in exasperation. "Last night you were positive you had seen him somewhere—or have you forgotten that?"

Leslie smiled. "Believe me, Drex Halloran isn't a man I'm likely to forget. It must have been wishful thinking on my part. So what are you going to do about him?"

"Why don't I invite him over, and the minute he enters the door, jump his bones?" L.C. regarded her friend glacially. "Does that meet with your approval?"

"Only if I'm allowed to watch." Leslie's eyes sparkled with teasing amusement.

The following day passed in a flurry of activity for L.C., as much mentally as physically.

Even though she'd met Drex Halloran only twice, she was fairly certain she would be hearing from him again.

She knew she'd be a hypocrite if she were to say she wasn't looking forward to that time. She was still young, and secretly yearned for the fulfillment that could only come from a gentle and understanding man, a man capable of restoring her flagging sense of sexual appeal. But the question that kept nagging at her during her class and later, as she hurried home, changed clothes, and rushed off to her new job, was whether or not she was capable of handling such a relationship.

Since that humiliating moment in the hospital when Charles had told her bluntly and without feeling that he was filing for divorce, she'd found herself vacillating between wanting a normal relationship with a man and wanting to inflict the kind of pain she'd known.

She sighed as she grasped the heavy handle of the glass door and entered the building where the law firm was located. Maybe Leslie was right; maybe she *did* have a grudge against men in general.

As she waited for the elevator, the ugly scene with her ex-husband ran through her mind. She'd been ill and in a state of deep depression when Charles had hurled his callous decision at her.

"Now?" she'd asked numbly. "You want a divorce now?"

"The baby was your idea, L.C.," he said without feeling. "You're the one who stopped taking the pill without telling me. You knew I wasn't ready for children."

"But I thought the baby—"

"You thought!" he said angrily. "It's always what you think. Accept it, L.C. We're about as far apart as two people can get. There's nothing left."

"Can't we at least try?" she'd whispered, not caring that she was degrading herself by begging. She had thought at the time that she couldn't live without Charles.

"Try?" he scoffed. "Don't be ridiculous. We're worlds apart. You're content with cheese and wine. I want champagne and caviar. If you really wanted our marriage to work, you'd stop refusing to accept help from that rich stepfather of yours," he added caustically.

"I can't ask Clayton for help." L.C. shook her head. "It would be embarrassing."

"But having a third divorce between you and your mother wouldn't be, right?"

"I guess not," L.C. murmured against the thickness gathering in her throat.

Charles turned and walked toward the door saying "My lawyer will get in touch with you." Then he was gone.

When the elevator doors opened, L.C. remained standing, staring emptily into space.

"Going up, miss?" an elderly gentleman asked, his finger on the open button.

59

"What?" she asked, startled, and then stepped forward, murmuring "Excuse me" beneath her breath.

By the time she reached her floor, L.C. had her thoughts and her emotions firmly under control. She reported to Brenda Foley and was taken to the typing pool, where she was introduced to the other typists, and was soon up to her neck in legal drafts. When five o'clock came, she covered her machine and, along with the other women, left the building and headed home.

She'd no more than put her key in the lock when she heard Leslie call her name. L.C. opened the door and stepped inside. "Is something wrong?" she yelled.

Leslie stuck her head around the kitchen door. "You have a telephone call. It's Louis."

L.C. dropped her purse on the sofa on her way to the kitchen. "Thanks, Les." She took the receiver. "Hi, Louis. What's up?"

The harassed voice of her employer at the detective agency filled her ear. "I need a favor."

"Oh?"

"I know it's short notice, but can you possibly do a little work for me this evening?"

"Louis," L.C. replied, "you know I'm swamped. I started that new job today, and I have to do some studying."

"I know, I know. But John had to go out of town on a case, and I'm shorthanded."

"Wasn't Sharon able to come in today?"

"Oh, it's not office work," he said quickly. "I need help with the Johnson case. Someone has to keep an eye on the place where Mr. Johnson's girlfriend lives. If you could just sit in your car and watch her apartment for three or four hours, it would give me time to meet with a new client, then relieve you. Can you do it?"

"You know I hate spying on people."

"Surveillance, L.C.," Louis corrected her. "It's called surveillance. Try to remember that Fred Johnson is a very wealthy man who's juggling a wife and two children and a mistress. Mrs. Johnson has put as many hours into their business as he has, and he's trying to shaft her."

"Point taken," L.C. said resignedly. "Are you sure I won't have to get out of the car?"

"Well . . ." Louis hesitated. "If they leave the girlfriend's apartment, you might have to tail them. But you can do it. Just stay back so you won't be recognized."

"All right, I'll do it. But there better be something extra in my pay envelope this week," L.C. warned, then hung up the receiver. She turned to a very interested Leslie. "I suppose you heard that?"

Her roommate grinned. "Even if I hadn't, Louis had already filled me in by the time you got home. Can you really do it?"

"I suppose so." L.C. frowned. "Just out of curiosity, I've gone out with John on stakeouts a few times." She started out of the kitchen, then stopped and turned back to Leslie. "Would you mind fixing me a sandwich and a thermos of coffee? Louis said he'd be along as soon as he finished with some new client, but he has a tendency to linger when he gets to talking."

An hour later L.C. was shifting restlessly behind the wheel of her car, not daring to take her eyes off the smart brick duplex. She was parked across the street from the woman's apartment, and was fully convinced that the life of a private investigator had to be the worst in the world.

Acting out of sheer boredom, she leaned forward to change the dial of the radio to another station. When she looked up again, she saw Fred Johnson getting out of a new Lincoln town car, a long florist box in one arm. The creep, L.C. thought viciously. How long had it been since he'd taken flowers home to his wife? She'd seen Sarah Johnson several times in the office and liked the woman. Her face showed the strain of living with a philandering husband, and her nerves were shot. The poor woman still loved the rat—though for the life of her L.C. couldn't figure out why —and didn't want a divorce.

A surge of rage swept over L.C. as she watched the tall, well-dressed man disappear into the apartment building. She truly hoped they were planning on an evening in, because she wasn't sure she could keep from running over the pair if they showed their faces. Her hopes were shattered. Within minutes she saw Fred and his mistress emerge from the building and head for the Lincoln.

CHAPTER FOUR

L.C. groaned with frustration. "Why the hell can't they stay in tonight?" She quickly started the engine. As soon as the Lincoln was on its way, her battered Chevy eased in behind.

The next thirty minutes were the most hectic of her life, L.C. decided as she slipped in and out of traffic in an attempt to keep the Lincoln in sight and at the same time not make it obvious that she was following it. There simply had to be an easier way of identifying that blasted car, she decided. She'd looked at so many taillights that she was beginning to think they were all the same.

Having assumed they were going to dinner, L.C. decided to really throw herself into the role of detective and try to figure out where they were headed. When they turned onto the bridge over the river, she gave a satisfied nod. She had a pretty good idea they were headed for LeRuth's, one of New Orleans's finest restaurants. She wondered how long it had been since that bum Johnson had taken his wife to such a nice place?

Several minutes later L.C. made the turn at the traffic light onto Franklin, then slipped into a parking place across the street from the restaurant. Once the lovebirds had gone inside, she reached underneath the front seat and pulled out a roll of orange fluorescent tape, left the Chevy, and made her way across the street to the row in the parking lot where she'd seen the Lincoln stop.

L.C. cast a furtive glance in all directions, then stepped behind the large, powerful car and went down on her knees, grimacing as the oyster-shelled surface bit through the thick cloth of her jeans. Without wasting a moment, she tore off two approximately one-inch squares of the tape and smoothed them against each outer edge of the taillight on the left rear. Another strip of tape was positioned in the center of the rear bumper, where it began to angle inward, toward the bottom of the car. She reared back as far as possible to observe her handiwork. Tailing Mr. Johnson would now be a piece of cake.

"That should do it," she murmured, pleased with the results.

"It definitely should."

Those three words, spoken in the relative quiet of the evening, made L.C. drop the roll of tape and swivel her head around to stare disbelievingly. It couldn't be! It simply couldn't be! Her sudden movement, and the

identity of the person who was directly behind her, leaning forward, his hands braced
on his thighs, caused her to land on her behind with her palms going down hard on the
oyster shells.

"What are you doing here?" L.C. all but
shrieked.

"I had a very enjoyable dinner and was
about to go home," Drex Halloran told her, a
heavy scowl lending a sinister look to his
craggy features. "Until now the evening has
gone relatively well. That is, until I came out
here and found a pint-sized vandal re-
arranging the design of the taillights on my
car."

"I'll have you know that this is not your
car," L.C. haughtily informed him. "I've followed this particular vehicle for miles." Dear
Lord, she was thinking wildly, why did she
have to meet him at this particular moment in
her life? "I am not a vandal."

"First of all, Miss Carlyle," Drex began in
his deep voice, "this very definitely is my car.
Second, applying tape to someone else's taillights is definitely vandalism." He remained
in his leaning position, and for the life of her
L.C. couldn't think of a single thing to say.

His car! He had said that, hadn't he? She sat
straighter in an attempt to see better, and
looked to the left and the right of "his" car.
Oh, God! She had been so sure! Her next
move was to lean far to her right and stare at
the license plate. She knew the numbers

didn't lie, but at that precise moment she wished with all her heart they did.

Well, she told herself as a sinking feeling washed over her, she'd really gone and done it this time. She took a deep breath and forced herself to look up at the angry man above her. "There really is an explanation for all of this, you know."

"I'd be pleased to hear it," Drex snapped, and for a moment L.C. was certain all his pearly white teeth were going to fall at her feet from the pressure exerted by his clenched jaws.

"I'm . . . um . . . I'm tailing someone."

"That fact alone should make that 'someone' very happy."

"There's no need to be nasty," she said with a glare. Funny, she thought, last night he seemed so different. He wasn't at all grumpy and irritated when he held her in his arms and kissed her.

"That, my dear Ms. Carlyle, depends on where you're standing. Let's hear the rest of the story," he demanded.

"Okay," she said briskly, "but would you mind stepping back? I don't like people hovering over me. We short people resent giants looming over us."

"My apologies," he icily replied. He reached down and grasped her under her arms and straightened, the force of his anger literally lifting L.C. off the ground so that her feet dangled in the air. Drex held her in this

67

embarrassing pose for a moment, then set her on her feet. "Continue."

L.C. gave a loud sniff of resentment, crossed her arms protectively across her upper body, then eyed him defiantly. "I work part-time for a detective agency."

"And?"

"One of the owners was out of town, and the other was tied up with a new client. I was asked to park across from a certain address and keep an eye on certain parties until my boss can relieve me. I had no idea it would be the night they decided to drive across the river for dinner."

"How does putting tape on my taillight fit into all this?" Drex asked, clearly baffled in spite of his initial anger.

L.C. shrugged. "I had a devil of a time keeping up with the people I was tailing, so I remembered something I'd seen on a TV show. They said if you wanted to tail a certain car, then try to attach some distinguishing mark on the taillights or the rear bumper. That way, it would stand out in traffic, making it easier to follow. Unfortunately, I hadn't counted on there being another car identical to Mr. Johnson's."

"May I ask what it is that 'Mr. Johnson' has done that would cause your agency to keep him under such close surveillance?" Drex asked.

"Mr. Johnson has the cute habit of playing around on his wife," L.C. bitterly informed

68

him. "Over the years they've built up a very profitable business, which he seems to enjoy sharing with the various women in his life while his wife and children sit home. He also wants a divorce, and prefers not to share his holdings with his family."

"And you, of course, disapprove of this."

"How would you like to be made a fool of, Mr. Halloran, by a person that you thought loved you? How would you like to have your pride trampled in the dirt? How would you like to be made a laughingstock before the whole world?"

Drex's gaze narrowed at the venom in her voice. In his profession he'd learned to read people by their voices, their gestures, and most of all by the glitter of revenge so often mirrored in their eyes. "Put like that, Ms. Carlyle, I don't suppose it would be very pleasant."

He bent down and retrieved the roll of tape, then walked over to the other Lincoln. L.C. watched in amazement as he calmly administered the same treatment to Johnson's taillight that she'd given his. When the job was done to his satisfaction, he took a step back, then turned and looked at an astonished L.C. " 'That should do it.' "

He walked back to where she was standing. "Now that that's taken care of, what do we do next?"

"We?" she croaked. Surely he wasn't planning on joining her for the remainder of the evening?

"Of course. New Orleans is a large city and I really don't think you should be out alone. I'm offering to keep you company until your boss shows up."

"Oh, but—No, you can't do that," she stammered.

"Why not? Do I have to have a special license?" he asked innocently.

"No," L.C. rushed on, "but I don't have any idea how long this will last. Louis isn't very reliable when it comes to being on time, and I don't have the slightest idea where the love-birds will go when they leave here. I really can't let you do this." While she was talking, she was pushing at her hair, the damp night air causing wispy tendrils to drop in a curling softness across her forehead. She was cursing herself for not having dressed with a bit more care. A baggy gray sweatshirt and jeans was hardly the sharpest outfit she could have worn. Thinking she would be sitting for hours in her car, she had merely put on comfortable clothes.

"In my business I'm accustomed to waiting for people, and I'd feel much better knowing you weren't alone," Drex insisted. He decided the matter by taking hold of her arm and leading her around to the passenger side of his car. "Suppose we sit here and wait for Mr. Johnson and his friend to appear? In the

70

meantime, we can decide what to do with your car while we tail him when they leave."

Her protests were brushed aside as easily as a few grains of unnecessary sand. Drex seated her in the car, then walked around and got in behind the wheel. He pressed a button and the seat went back further than it already was. The steering wheel was tilted out of his way, and L.C. wouldn't have been at all surprised if a king-size bed had suddenly materialized.

"Very nice," she murmured in confusion at her thoughts. Why was she thinking of beds in connection with Drex Halloran?

"I'm glad you like it."

L.C. turned to look over her shoulder at the door of the restaurant, only to find her view partially blocked by the back of the seat and the padded headrest. How in the world was she going to keep an eye on the entrance of the restaurant if she had to peep through cracks or crane her neck like a flamingo?

Suddenly the quiet whirr caught her ear again, and the seat she was sitting in became a plush recliner with the back sufficiently low for her to see over it without straining. Now she was positive there was a bed in the damn car, and she wasn't in the least comfortable with the idea.

"Thank you," she managed to say without looking at Drex, her eyes glued to the front of the restaurant.

Drex merely nodded, then turned so that

his back was against the door. One arm rested on the steering wheel, the other on the edge of the seat.

"How often do you do this sort of thing?" he asked. After his initial spurt of anger at seeing someone tampering with his car, and his surprise that it was L.C., he couldn't believe his luck. Though he still couldn't figure out what it was about her that fascinated him, he had no intention of letting this opportunity slip by. She'd gotten away from him last night, but this time was different. Not only were they alone, under rather unusual circumstances, but he also had her address and telephone number, thanks to her roommate.

"Er . . . actually, this is my first time alone," L.C. was loathe to admit. She'd acted like a rank amateur—which she was, but she hated to let Drex Halloran know it. "I went out a couple of times with John, the other partner in the firm, but he really did all the work. I'm one of their part-time secretaries."

"Leslie told me last night that you're in law school."

"Yes, I am. Third year."

"Is this job your only one? I seem to remember your roommate saying something about you working more than one job?"

The answer came automatically to her lips, but before she spoke, L.C. paused. "Has anyone ever told you that you're incredibly nosey?" She heard that soft chuckle she'd come to associate with him, remembering the feel of it reverberating from deep within his chest.

"I'm interested. Does that bother you?"

"It would bother me less if I knew the reason behind your interest."

Drex stared thoughtfully at her, and L.C. found herself fidgeting beneath his penetrating gaze. "Taking you to bed is the main reason behind my interest. I think it would be nice."

"You think?" The words exploded from L.C.'s lips before she could stop them. "Are you in the habit of trying out your women, then throwing them back like fish if they don't satisfy you?" Lord, he was nervy!

"Something like that," he admitted glibly. "It reduces the stress and tension in a relationship."

"Stress and tension," L.C. murmured dazedly. "How considerate of you. Is it difficult finding women willing to go along with your . . . plans?"

"So far they've all cooperated beautifully," he replied, his lips twitching humorously.

"And now you're ready to grant me the honor?" L.C. asked sweetly, seeing nothing amusing about his amoral behavior or the fact that she should be basking in the limelight of his attention.

"Absolutely."

"When did you make this decision?"

"The first time I saw you."

"You're sick!"

73

"You didn't think so last night just before your conscience reminded you of your friend Vic," Drex patiently reminded her.

"Vic means a great deal to me." She gave him a flinty-eyed look.

"You should never tell lies, L.C. When you do a greenish hue creeps over your lovely face. By the way, what does L.C. stand for?"

"Laurin Catherine, and my face is not green," she snapped. One hand began fumbling for the door handle.

"No," he agreed, "it's almost back to its normal color. Laurin Catherine is a beautiful name. Why don't you use it? You can also stop trying to get out of the car, the locks are controlled from a panel behind me. Besides, you really don't want to get away from me, and you know it."

L.C. stopped her frantic search and whirled around to stare at him. "You are incredible," she said slowly. "It's my fervent hope that the next woman you proposition will bash you over the head with a meat cleaver."

She saw him move, but short of scrambling over the back of the seat like some sort of beetle, there was very little she could do. His arms plucked her from her seat and settled her in his lap before she could utter more than a breathless "Don't you dare!"

"I don't like arguing with you, Laurin Catherine, and I especially don't like you all the way across the seat from me," she was calmly told. His arm curled around the back of her shoulders, providing a perfect cushion for her neck, while the other one dropped across her thighs, his hand clasped to the pivotal point of her hip.

"I'm an expert in karate," L.C. gasped against sensuous lips that were slowly gaining a response from her rigid ones.

"Good," Drex whispered seductively, nipping and tasting at her mouth. "I like a little kinky sex every once in a while. Variety, you know."

"Relieves tension and stress, no doubt," L.C. whispered as the tip of his tongue teased its way into her mouth.

Desire exploded inside her veins like thousands of tiny bubbles, causing a slight trembling in her body, which Drex felt. His arms tightened like bands of steel, his mouth doing erotic things to hers, his lips teasing and plundering until L.C. was clutching his shoulders for support, afraid she would be swept away in the whirlpool sucking her closer and closer into its swirling middle.

Large capable hands, more gentle than she could ever have imagined, slipped beneath the roomy fullness of her sweatshirt and boldly stroked the tender sides of her breasts. L.C. couldn't control the tiny expression of exquisite pleasure that tore from her lips at the sensation. She arched her upper body closer to that touch, impatient to have those hands stroking not only her breasts but the rest of her as well.

The sound of voices, one petulant and whiny, made Drex lift his head and listen. After a moment or two he looked back down at L.C., a soft smile of tenderness on his hard face as he saw the mixture of passion and bewilderment in his mystery lady's face. "I could quite easily consign your Mr. Johnson and his mistress to hell." He dipped his head and touched his lips to her burning cheek. "Is it really necessary for you to continue this spying mission?"

CHAPTER FIVE

L.C. wasn't sure she would be able to take her roommate's gloating look of "I told you so" when she reached the apartment with her friend in tow. Leslie would be pleased as punch at how the evening was turning out. L.C. could almost see her friend's blue eyes gleaming with curiosity as she impatiently waited for all the juicy details.

L.C. took her eyes off the road for a moment and threw a hurried look into the rearview mirror. The headlights of the Lincoln were still behind her. The larger car wasn't exactly riding the bumper of the Chevy, but it would have been impossible for another vehicle to slip into the narrow space between them; Drex was making sure of that.

He'd also taken care to remind L.C.—again —that she was anything but impervious to his lovemaking. She raised a hand, the tips of her fingers gently brushing against the still swollen tenderness of her lips. Drex Halloran was a master when it came to seduction, she told herself. Twice she'd been in his arms, and twice she'd emerged trembling and wary, but feeling some inexplicable sense of completion as well. He'd also been perfectly candid when he'd told her he wanted to go to bed with her. Never had a man been so blunt and open with her.

The hand touching her lips slipped around to cup her nape as she again concentrated on her driving. Trying to figure out the workings of a mind like Drex Halloran's was a challenge for L.C., one that she was beginning to find extremely fascinating.

The moment the apartment door opened and Leslie saw Drex, it was all L.C. could do to keep from laughing at the expression on her friend's face. Leslie considered herself a connoisseur of men, and in her opinion Drex Halloran was one of the finest of his kind floating around.

"What a nice surprise," Leslie drawled, her eyes twinkling with amusement as she watched L.C. and their guest enter the living room. "I don't recall telling you where you could find her when you called earlier. How did you manage it?" she asked Drex.

"Simple," he grinned expansively. "Your roommate found me—or rather my car. After having dinner with friends, I came out of the restaurant and found her crouched behind my car, calmly taping one of my taillights."

"Were you really?" Leslie looked curiously at L.C. "Why were you doing that?"

L.C.'s mouth was set with annoyance as she

looked from one to the other. "I was bored," she airily replied. "You should try it sometime, Les. Defacing other people's property is really a neat way to relieve tension."

"It's pressure," Leslie said decisively, immediately coming to her roommate's defense. "What with law school and two jobs, L.C. has taken on far too much, Drex. I'm sure her insurance will cover whatever damages have been done to your car."

"Oh, but I have no intention of filing a claim, Leslie," Drex said pleasantly. "I'm sure Laurin Catherine can work out something that will be agreeable to both of us."

"Who?" Leslie asked, puzzled.

"Laurin Catherine, Les." L.C. favored her roommate with a saccharine smile. "Have you forgotten what a lovely name I have?"

"Er—no. No, of course not," Leslie muttered, clearly at a loss to understand what was going on. She gave Drex a faint smile, looked questioningly at L.C. one last time, then began edging toward the hall. "There's a fresh pot of coffee if you'd like some. There are also a couple of sandwiches," she added, then turned and scurried from the room.

"You have a very devoted friend," Drex remarked. He removed the jacket of the dark suit he was wearing and tossed it on a chair, then loosened his tie. "Weren't you rather harsh with her?"

"She is a very good friend, and I was harsh because she enjoys trying to run my life. Why

79

are you taking off your clothes?" L.C. regarded him warily.

"Jacket. I've only removed my jacket," he pointed out as though explaining it to a child. He walked over and sat down on the sofa, then leaned back, perfectly at ease. He patted the cushion beside him. "Won't you join me?"

"I have to study." But in spite of what she knew she should be doing, L.C. found herself joining him.

"Are you always this argumentative?" Drex asked, noting the distance she'd deliberately put between them. "Is there something about me that just naturally sets you on edge? One minute you're warm and very human. The next, you're the original ice maiden."

L.C. winced at the words. She'd heard similar comments from Charles during their short marriage. But as a wife her defense was that her husband hadn't exactly been the most considerate man when it came to making love. His gratification was all that interested him. If L.C. happened to gain some small measure of satisfaction, it was purely an accident. She quickly came to realize that her husband's strong sexual urge was just that—a nightly urge, without a thought or care for her needs or wants. Naturally she'd become withdrawn and unresponsive, and Charles had become more abusive as time went on.

"Is that how you really see me?" she asked, recalling Charles's favorite taunt. In some of his uglier moments he had remarked that

80

making love to her was like holding a block of ice in his arms.

"Not all the time. When I've held you in my arms and kissed you you've responded like the warm, sensual woman I think you are. But the moment I release you, you throw up that guard and try to freeze me out."

"I really don't know you very well."

Drex slowly shook his head. "That's not even a passable excuse, Laurin," he said. "Try again."

"Maybe I'm not in the mood to 'try again,'" she told him. "And I prefer to be called L.C."

"Then be yourself," Drex suggested. "The way you were last night when you slipped away from the dance and took off your shoes. That was natural and uninhibited. It was *you*. And I happen to prefer the name Laurin. L.C. brings to mind someone masculine, and you're definitely not masculine. You're a very lovely woman."

"Ice and all?" She grinned.

"I don't remember anything icy last night about the woman I carried in my arms, then later kissed." He continued staring at her. "Who turned you off sex, Laurin Catherine Carlyle?"

"You mean you didn't learn everything about me from your lengthy conversation with Leslie?" she asked cheekily.

"Ah, you resent that, do you?"

"Of course. Wouldn't you?"

"Absolutely not," Drex smiled. "Ask me anything you want."

"What does Drex Halloran do when he isn't attending carnival balls?"

"I'm an attorney."

"You are?" L.C. drew her feet beneath her and turned so that she was facing him. No wonder he was so good at asking questions. "What's your speciality?"

"Personal injury. I occasionally take on something else, but not very often. Anything else?"

"The first time we met, you said something about having an apartment here in New Orleans. Have you recently moved here?"

"My home is in Houston, but I'm associated with a firm here. Since the case I'm working on now looks to be a long, drawn-out affair, it seemed logical to find some place other than a hotel room."

"What about your practice in Houston?"

"I divide my time between the two cities."

"Oh," L.C. murmured thoughtfully. She wondered if he also divided his time between the women of Houston and New Orleans as well. He hadn't been bashful about mentioning that women were his main source of entertainment.

"No, Ms. Carlyle, I don't have a mistress stashed away, so you can put that thought out of your mind," Drex inserted smoothly.

"It was just a thought," L.C. said defensively. Damn him! Not only was he a roving tomcat, he was a mind reader to boot. "Would you like some coffee?" Now why did she say that?

"I was wondering when you'd remember your manners," Drex teased. "Do you need any help?"

"No," L.C. said crisply as she got to her feet. She didn't want him hovering over her while she poured coffee. She'd probably do something else meaningful—like scalding him!

As she prepared the tray in the kitchen, she found herself going over each thing she knew about Drex Halloran. She remembered her own thoughts two days ago when she wondered whether or not she should attempt to seduce him. Ha! That was a laugh. So far he'd done the seducing and she hadn't done a single thing to stop him. It wasn't ice in her veins that made her throw up her guard, she decided; it was the fear of falling for him just as she'd done with Charles.

When she returned to the living room, Drex was standing in front of the built-in bookcase studying the eclectic reading material.

"I'm afraid you won't find anything very interesting there," L.C. remarked. "Neither Les nor I have very much time for reading."

"Where do you plan to practice when you finish school?" Drex asked. He walked back over to the sofa and sat down beside her. Only this time he sat in the middle.

"Here in the city, I suppose. Hopefully I'll

be hired by a firm. I've been told that young lawyers on their own usually starve to death. The part-time job I started today is in the typing pool of a rather large firm. Who knows? Maybe when I pass the bar I can work with them."

"Which firm is that?"

"Grimaldi and a long list of associates. Are you familiar with them?"

"Quite. It's a very reputable firm. I happen to know, however, that they deal mostly in personal injury and corporate law," Drex informed her. He refused cream or sugar for his coffee, sipping the hot brew in spite of the steam curling from the cup. "I'm afraid they don't handle very many divorces."

"How did you know that's what I'm interested in?"

"A simple matter of deduction, Laurin. When you were telling me about that Johnson fellow earlier, your eyes were like fiery emeralds. Leslie mentioned you were divorced, so"—he regarded her closely—"it seemed the most logical conclusion. What happened in your marriage to make you so bitter?"

"I'd rather not talk about it," L.C. said quietly. She placed the cup and saucer on the table in front of the sofa and sat forward, her face expressionless. "I hate to be rude, but it is late."

She heard his expansive sigh as Drex returned his cup to the tray, then felt his hands on her arms, turning her to face him. "I don't give a damn if I have to sit here until the sun warps the paint on the walls, sweetheart, I'm not about to leave until I get some answers," he countered in a hard, determined voice. His gaze was as relentless as his grip on her arms, and L.C. was unable to stop the shiver that snaked its way over her body.

"I'm the original ice maiden, remember? Why bother?" she taunted in an attempt to draw her own measure of blood.

A quickly administered shake that almost gave her whiplash was all she got for her trouble. "All right, my remarks were a bad play on words, and I'm sorry. Okay? You've obviously been told that before by some uncaring bastard that couldn't start a flame in a roomful of dynamite with a case of matches, much less a warm, sensitive woman. But that's behind you—or is it?"

"It is to the extent that I don't lie awake all night thinking about it anymore, but my thoughts aren't that easily controlled," L.C. said quietly. "My father deserted my mother and my brother and me when I was three years old. Later in my life, when I was foolish enough to think I'd found the one man in this world who really cared for me, I lost the baby I was carrying and was asked by my husband for a divorce all in a few days. I'm afraid you'll have to forgive me if there are times when the practiced lines you and other men use fail to impress me. The men closest to me, other than my brother, turned out to be duds."

"Is that what you really think I'm doing, shooting you a line of bull?" Drex growled.

"Isn't it?"

"No. If you recall, I haven't promised a single thing or asked for anything from you. I've been perfectly honest in telling you that I desire you . . . that I want you."

"Is that supposed to make you extra special?"

"Well it damn sure beats the hell out of pretending to be in love with you."

"Which you're not."

"No. I'm very attracted to you. I want to be with you, get a chance to know you better. But at the moment love doesn't enter into it," Drex stated bluntly.

"You certainly go to a lot of trouble for attraction's sake." L.C. was forced to smile. She had to admit that what he said was true. He had been open about wanting to go to bed with her. Surely that counted for something . . . didn't it?

"I'm accustomed to going to a lot of trouble in my profession. I'm also a stickler for detail," Drex stated with a dark, intense stare. "And when I see a beautiful woman *attempting* to have a good time the first two times I see her, it interests me."

"Was I so obvious?"

"Only to someone used to reading people. Your friend Vic hasn't caught on yet." His hands on her arms transferred their hold to her waist and hauled her onto his lap. "This is becoming a habit." But his own thoughts were far from calm. God! She must have been married to a genuine bastard. What kind of man could desert his wife when she'd just lost their baby? A feeling of rage rushed through Drex, rage and a strong desire to protect the woman he was holding in his arms.

At the moment L.C. found no fault with the seating arrangement. For, whatever else he was or wasn't, Drex Halloran had the power to do strange and wondrous things to her emotions. Things she didn't find offensive in the least.

"I didn't know you'd lost a baby," he said softly against her hair. "That must have hurt like hell." As he spoke, his hands had slipped beneath the edge of the gray sweatshirt she was wearing and were running over her body like large soothing blankets of heat. There were no sexual overtones in his caresses, merely the healing ministrations of touch—of slightly callused palms against a softer, more delicate surface.

To L.C. the gentleness emanating from this man was as much a surprise as the powerful desire he could so easily arouse in her. He was truly an enigma. But enigma or not, when he caught her chin and forced her head back, and when his lips claimed hers, L.C. wouldn't have cared if he were Satan himself. Tiny embers of need were swiftly fanned into glowing coals of passion as their tongues met, drew back, and then began an erotic dance that swept everything from her mind but the curling spirals of desire creeping over her.

Her hands went to his head, her fingers burying themselves in the crisp darkness of his hair. She wanted to touch him, wanted to know the texture of his skin beneath her fingertips. Beneath her thighs she could feel the hard arousal of his body pressing against her and knew a moment of incredible excitement. She felt the same surge of power as she had that night on the terrace outside the ballroom when she'd felt the trembling of his large body as he'd kissed her. She wasn't cold and frigid. When cold, frigid women were kissed, they didn't utter low, husky sounds of pleasure as she was doing now, or feel slow, languorous tremors attacking their limbs.

CHAPTER SIX

The door of the bathroom opened and Leslie strolled in, holding an enormous bouquet of yellow roses, a huge grin on her face. "I wish I owned the flower shop where Drex has his account. Where do you want me to put these?"

"What's left?" L.C. asked after she finished brushing her teeth. Within the last few days their apartment had taken on the look of a hothouse. One to two bouquets of flowers were delivered daily.

"The kitchen or the bathroom."

"Not in here please," L.C. grinned. "Put them in the kitchen. When I see him tonight, I'll try to persuade him to put an end to this madness."

"Why on earth would you do that?"

"Because I'm getting a headache from all the different scents. We can't move around here without stumbling over a bouquet."

"You could suggest something a little more substantial," Leslie suggested.

"Such as?" L.C. regarded her narrowly.

"Oh . . . a diamond bracelet or some other little trinket."

"In exchange for what?"

"A long weekend in Acapulco or Cancún would be nice."

"Why don't I just move in with him for a few weeks?"

"Great!" Leslie exclaimed. "Do you want me to help you pack?"

"Really!" L.C. shook her head disgustedly. "When will you get it through your head that I have to do things in my own good time? And right now I'm not ready to have an affair with Drex Halloran. Lord, Leslie, he's light years ahead of me in experience. He's spent a lifetime perfecting his craft of seduction. Have pity—please. Let me find some nice, easygoing man who's as unsure of himself as I am."

Leslie grimaced. "That statement leaves me nauseous," she said. "Easygoing indeed!"

L.C. left the bathroom and headed for her bedroom. At the door she turned and smiled saucily. "If you'll excuse me, I would like to get dressed—alone." She slammed the door, then laughed when she heard the off-key sound of her roommate's voice raised in song.

But as she dressed for dinner with Drex, L.C. knew that sooner or later she would have to make a decision regarding their relationship. His intentions were obvious; he made no effort to hide them. He wanted her. She couldn't help but smile as she remembered parts of their time together the last few days.

One evening when she'd gotten into his car, she's noticed a peculiar-looking piece of equipment wrapped in a clear plastic bag lying next to him on the front seat. "What's that?" she'd asked.

"An acetylene torch," he'd replied with a perfectly straight face.

"What's it for?"

"Later in the evening."

"Are you planning on cutting through something?" she asked, puzzled.

"Yes. That damn twelve-inch wall of ice around your heart." He had looked over at her and grinned. "Think it will do the trick?"

"How cowardly!" L.C. lifted her chin and sniffed. "A real man wouldn't have to stoop to such tactics."

"I'll remind you of that when you start floundering like a fish, looking for a way out."

"You do have the most remarkable ways of expressing yourself."

"I was hoping you'd notice."

Another time, while taking a drive after a long, leisurely dinner, L.C. found herself perspiring. Even though it was still February, the temperature wasn't all that cool outside, but it was stifling inside the car.

"Is something wrong with your air conditioning?" she said as she pulled at the neck of her dress.

"No," Drex assured her.

"There has to be," she argued. "It's at least ninety degrees in this car."

91

"I know."

"Well, aren't you warm?"

"About to go up in smoke."

"Then do something."

"I'd love to, Laurin darling, but you're the most uncooperative woman I've ever met."

She gave him a sizzling look. "Do you mean you've been practically roasting me alive just to pull one of your practical jokes?"

"Who's joking?" Drex looked at her, his warm gaze sweeping over her in such a suggestive manner she felt as though she didn't have on a stitch of clothing. "I've turned into a damned prune from cold showers since I met you. I keep hoping I'll find whatever it is that turns you on."

"You turn me on, Drex," L.C. was astonished to hear herself admitting. It was a ridiculous conversation and she knew it, but five minutes in his company had her doing and saying things she would never have done with another man.

"There are turn-ons and there are turn-ons, sweetheart," he drawled huskily. "Until I get the right one, I'll just have to keep on reminding you that sex between a man and a woman can be a beautiful thing."

And he had kept on, L.C. mused as she picked up the soft brush and applied blush to her cheeks. He'd sent flowers daily. There had been a singing telegram, delivered by a freckle-faced college student who blushed when he sang the slightly ribald song given him by the gentleman who had looked as tough as nails. Leslie had doubled over with laughter, and L.C. was as mad as a hornet when said gentleman appeared at her door several hours later.

Finished with her makeup, L.C. walked over to the bed and picked up her dress. It was made of a soft, clingy material in a deep rose, another of Leslie's little finds for her. The bodice, while not quite as revealing as the dress she'd worn to the carnival ball, was still so plunging as to preclude the use of a bra.

Just as she sprayed a quick touch of perfume to her neck and wrist, L.C. heard the doorbell. She tipped her head to one side and listened. In seconds the sound of Drex's voice could be heard in low conversation with Leslie. Two masters of the art of conniving in the same room. That would never do. She scooped up her small clutch and a light wrap, then hurried to join them.

Drex's gaze was trained on the door, and the moment L.C. entered the living room, she felt its lambent gleam caressing the dusky hollow between her breasts.

Leslie looked at her friend approvingly. "I was just telling Drex how lovely all the flowers are. Don't you think so, L.C.?"

"I've already told him how pretty they are." She turned to Drex. "You're early."

"Sue me," he said silkily. "I was anxious to see you."

"Oh," L.C. murmured, embarrassed by the raw desire she saw glowing in his dark eyes.

Leslie looked from one to the other, making no effort to mask her approval or amusement.

"Shall we go?" Drex offered softly. He smiled at Leslie, then reached out and slipped a hand beneath L.C.'s elbow and ushered her out the door.

"Do you have to do that?" she asked the moment they were alone.

"Do what?" Drex asked innocently.

"Make it so obvious that you . . . er . . ."

"That I enjoy looking at your body? That I want to go to bed with you?" he finished for her.

"I suppose so," she grumbled as she walked toward his car. "It's embarrassing. By your looks and the way you act, you give the impression that we're already sleeping together."

Drex caught her shoulders and turned her to him, his expression as he looked down at her hard and unyielding. "That's exactly what I want people to think."

"Why?"

"Because it will tell other men that you're off limits. You belong to me."

L.C. stamped her foot in frustration. "I don't belong to you, Drex Halloran," she stormed.

"Don't you?" He smiled, then bent his head and kissed her hard and swiftly, one hand eas-

94

ing down to cup the fullness of one rigid-tipped breast. Beneath it he could feel the rapid beating of her heart. "Then why is your heart suddenly racing? Why have your eyes turned to soft green pools?"

"Humidity," L.C. replied in a strangled voice.

"Liar," he chuckled, then opened the door for her.

L.C. stared straight ahead as he rounded the front of the car and got in. Damn him! Didn't he ever give up? Then again, was she sure she wanted him to?

As Drex eased the car into the fast-moving traffic, L.C. sat stiffly, refusing to bend an inch. Being with him every single evening was beginning to make her a nervous wreck. What with kisses that were slowly proving to her that they alone weren't enough, his not-so-subtle innuendoes regarding their relationship, and his comical escapades, she felt like she'd been leveled by a steamroller.

"I have to be out of town for a couple of days on business," Drex said, breaking the heavy silence. "I'd like you to come with me."

"Just like that?" L.C. glowered at him. "Have you forgotten that I'm in school and that I also have to work for a living?"

"Not at all. I think it's a very courageous thing you're doing, and I admire you. Now," he asked levelly, "will you come with me?"

L.C. opened her mouth to rebuke him, then just as quickly closed it. Why bother?

Drex had an infuriating way of twisting everything she said. "No."

"Dammit!" he exploded with such force L.C. jumped two inches off the seat. "Just how long are you going to grieve after that stupid son of a bitch you were married to?" His anger was transferred to his driving, causing him to suddenly swerve out and pass the car they'd been following, then cut back in front with only inches to spare, bringing a sharp blare of the horn from the irate driver.

"I am not grieving for Charles!" L.C. yelled. "Even if I were, it's no concern of yours."

"I'm beginning to get very tired of the way you think, Laurin Catherine," he snapped. "You're not a nun. You haven't taken a vow of chastity—I don't think," he added grudgingly. "Yet you run from your emotions like a frightened child. Are you afraid that if you really let go of that huge grudge against all men you're carrying, you might find one of us who isn't going to hurt you?"

"Just think, all of this because I won't go to bed with you." She hooted derisively.

Drex shot her a nasty glare. "Are you secretly lusting after your precious Vic?" he asked stingingly.

"You're sick."

"You've told me that before."

"Then by now you should believe me."

"How can I do that, sweetheart, when you haven't been honest with me a single time since we met?"

L.C. had no ready answer, and Drex didn't push her. He seemed as weary as she from their exchange of words. For some reason he couldn't fathom, he'd become obsessed with Laurin Catherine Carlyle. No other woman he'd ever known had caused his mind to wander during the preparation of a trial—but Laurin had. He couldn't remember wanting to spend all his evenings with a woman who promised nothing more at the end than a kiss, but that's how he felt about Laurin. He found himself consumed with hatred for the husband that had treated her so shabbily. The baby she'd lost pulled at Drex, leaving him with the most peculiar urge to see her pregnant with his child.

Love and marriage were two things Drex had shied away from for years, he mused as he drove. Being raised in an orphanage had instilled within him a strong instinct for survival. Once on his own, he'd begun preparations for the career he'd decided on when he was ten years old. His lips curved into a grim smile. Power and wealth had been the two primary goals that saw him through years of washing dishes and whatever other odd jobs came his way as he fought and scratched his way through college and law school.

"May I share the joke?" L.C. asked quietly. This was the first time Drex had remained quiet for so long after one of their spats, and it bothered her.

"Are you sure you want to?" He grinned.

"Of course."

"I was plotting the best way to get you alone with me for two days."

"You're incorrigible."

"I know, but a certain sexy little brunette who is as stubborn as hell affects me that way."

Dinner was enjoyable, and passed without Drex mentioning his upcoming trip again. In fact, he didn't mention it at all. When he took L.C. home, he refused to come in, saying he still had some work to do. His good-night kiss had her slim, supple body molding itself to his stronger one like a hand fitting into a well-worn glove.

"You do believe in taking advantage of a situation, don't you, sweetheart?" he rasped in an agonized voice as he raised his head and stared down at her. His hands went to her waist and pulled her intimately against his thighs, and L.C. trembled. "Can you feel what you do to me?" he asked hoarsely.

L.C. could, only this time she wasn't feeling victorious. Her own body was crying out for fulfillment just as sharply as his. "Give me time, Drex. Please?"

"By the time you make up your mind, sweetheart, I'll be floating down the shower drain with the cold water." He smiled then, the gentleness in him warming her heart. "I'll give you a little more time—but only a little more."

After he'd gone, she leaned her back

against the door and let the room slowly right itself. Drex's lovemaking was becoming more and more difficult to handle, as was her own desire for him.

"It's for you, L.C." Mary, a young housewife working to help put her husband through medical school, smiled as she reached across her desk and handed L.C. the phone.

"Thanks, Mary," L.C. murmured, then grinned at the faint rumblings coming from her stomach. It was five past twelve and she was ravenous. She placed the receiver to her ear. "Hello?"

"L.C.? Brenda here. I need to ask a big favor of you. Can you possibly come to my office for a few minutes?"

"Sure, Brenda. I'll be right there."

"What's the problem?" she asked a few moments later as she faced a harassed Brenda.

"The flu is the biggest problem. We've got three secretaries out, and everyone looking to me to provide instant relief." She waved L.C. to a chair. "Please—sit."

"What can I do to help?"

"Some member of the firm—whichever one can get loose first—has to fly to the northern part of the state this afternoon to take a statement from a witness in an off-shore drilling accident. Would you be willing to fill in for his secretary, who's out sick?"

L.C. shrugged. "I suppose so. Who will I be accompanying?"

"At the moment I'm not certain."

"Are you sure he won't be upset with a mere typist?"

"Honey, at this stage of the game, you'll be welcomed with open arms," Brenda assured her. "You'll need to be at the airport at one o'clock sharp. You can get cab money from petty cash. Can you make it?"

L.C. assured her she could, then took the location of the hangar and the time of departure and left. Back at her desk she tried to call Leslie to tell her she would be late coming home. Her roommate was at lunch, however, so L.C. left word with the receptionist. After that had been taken care of, she freshened her hair and makeup, stopped at petty cash, and caught a cab to the airport.

After paying the taxi driver, L.C. hitched the strap of her shoulder bag and headed for the office of the small airfield. There was a strong wind, and her hair was blowing around her face. There were a number of small planes tied down beyond the runway, and she eyed them with misgiving. She'd never flown in a small plane and wasn't looking forward to it.

"I'm L.C. Carlyle," she told the friendly-looking young man behind the counter. "I'm supposed to be meeting someone here from the Grimaldi law firm at one o'clock. Do you know if they've arrived yet?"

"Sure thing, Ms. Carlyle. I was expecting

you," she was told. "See that blue and white Piper Navajo out there on your right?"

L.C. squinted against the glare of sun on the runways, her gaze following the man's direction. "The one parked in front of that hangar?"

"That's it. Just go through that door"—he nodded toward the back of the office—"and keep on walking, then get on board. The plane's all ready to go."

Just as L.C. walked around the front of the plane she got the surprise of her life. Drex emerged from the hangar and was walking toward her.

"What are you doing here?" she asked, one hand going to her hair and attempting to smooth it.

"Waiting for you." Drex flashed her a smile, then bent down and kissed her.

"Waiting for me?" she frowned. "I'm afraid I don't understand."

"Aren't you suppose to be going with a member of your firm to the northern part of the state?" he asked.

"Yes, I am." L.C. looked thoughtful for a moment. "But how did you know?"

He grinned. "Because I'm that member."

L.C. stared at him as if he'd suddenly gone mad. "You mean you're one of that long list of attorneys associated with the firm?" There was a sharpness in her voice that left Drex in little doubt of her displeasure.

"In a way."

"What way?"

"It's my firm."

"What about Matthew Grimaldi?"

"My former partner, now deceased. For business reasons it would have been foolish to change the name."

"You must really be proud of yourself," L.C. said stingingly.

"I am," Drex replied silkily. "I really wanted you to come on this trip with me, and Brenda agreed to go along with my plan." He reached out and caught her elbow. "Shall we get started?"

"What else have you conveniently forgotten to tell me?" she asked stonily, refusing to budge one inch. As a matter of fact, she thought maliciously, she wasn't at all sure she would even go with him. She'd quit jobs before, and she could just as easily leave this one. "Did you also lie about being single?"

"I haven't lied to you about anything, Ms. Carlyle," Drex ground out. "Knowing how paranoid you are about getting involved with any man, I knew that if I confessed to having any connections with the firm, much less being your boss, I'd never see you again." He released her arm long enough to push back his cuff and glance at his watch. "We'll have to finish this conversation while we're flying." He whipped an arm around L.C.'s waist and half pushed, half carried her the few feet to the plane.

L.C.'s face was a study of contradictions as

102

she sat silent and rebellious in the copilot's seat while Drex talked to the tower. He hadn't really lied to her, she reasoned sourly, but neither had he bothered to inform her of all the facts. Suddenly the name Halloran began tugging at her memory for an entirely different reason. Surely not, she scoffed. She turned and regarded him coolly. "I suppose you'll be telling me next that you aren't at all related to the H. D. Halloran who's written two textbooks on the subjects of contracts and evidence."

"Not at all," Drex answered calmly, not bothering to look up from the panel of switches and buttons he was working like an expert. "I plead guilty on both counts."

"But . . . but . . ." L.C. spluttered, the jab backfiring on her. "I assumed H. D. Halloran was an old man."

He grinned, amused by her nonplussed state. "Thirty-eight might seem ancient to you, Laurin, but I assure you I'm not in my dotage yet."

L.C. made no reply. Instead, she watched him lean over and check her seat belt, the scent of him bringing uncomfortable memories of being in his arms and enjoying it— before she knew what a deceitful wretch he was!

CHAPTER SEVEN

For the first hour of the trip L.C. sat like a clam beside Drex, offering nothing more than an occasional nod to the conversation he seemed determined to carry on.

She had the right to be angry, she kept telling herself. He'd deceived her, and she wasn't feeling the least forgiving.

When she felt the full brunt of his gaze resting on her, she shifted uncomfortably in her seat, wishing they were in a car so that he would be forced to pay attention to the traffic rather than her.

"Would you care for something to drink?" Drex asked cheerfully. The question was followed by the brush of his fingertips against her throat.

L.C. stiffened at his touch. "No, thank you." She primly lifted her chin a fraction of an inch higher and stared straight ahead.

"How about a sandwich?"

"No, thank you."

"How about a kiss?"

"Drop dead."

"No, thank you," Drex chuckled. "Your neck is going to start hurting, you know."

"Oh?" L.C. turned her head and regarded him haughtily. "Have you also been hiding a medical degree?"

"Not at all, sweetheart, but even I know you can't continue to keep that stubborn little chin so high in the air without getting a cramp in your neck."

"Your concern is touching."

"I can see that you're really impressed by it. Tell me something, Laurin"—Drex was suddenly very serious—"what's really bothering you? I find it hard to believe that you'd be this angry just because I failed to tell you of my connections with the firm."

"I dislike being lied to," she said moodily.

"Which I haven't done," he pointed out. "I simply omitted to fill you in on all the details."

"It's the same difference," she stubbornly maintained.

"If you'd known it was my firm you were working for, would you have resigned?"

"I'm—not sure," she said. "But at least I would have been able to make that decision on my own. The way things are now, I feel like I've been tricked."

"Have I in any way interfered with you and the performance of your duties at the firm?" Drex asked. As much as it galled her, L.C. shook her head. "Then I fail to see the reason behind this pouting session you're indulging in."

"I'm not pouting," she flared, not wanting to admit even the tiniest bit that he had a point. "I'm simply disagreeing with you."

"Exactly how long do you plan to stay in your present disagreeable state?"

"I haven't decided," she replied frostily, though it was getting harder and harder to keep from giving in to his gentle persuasion.

"I love the way your eyes are glowing right now," Drex said huskily. "And your lips are in the most delightful pout. I'd love to kiss you."

L.C. could feel the rush of color stinging her cheeks as he continued to make love to her without even touching her. He was so adept at his craft, she thought in defeat, it was impossible to stay mad at him. "Do—Don't you think you should pay more attention to where we're going?" she stammered, knowing she'd lost the battle the moment she allowed her gaze to become entangled with his.

"That's what automatic pilots are for."

"Oh," L.C. murmured, looking sharply ahead as though expecting to see a huge 747 jet bearing down on them.

"Don't worry," Drex said with an easy laugh. He caught her clenched fist and gently intertwined his fingers with hers. "Relax. We're in no danger."

"I've never flown in a small plane before."

"Do you like it?"

"I'm not sure. How long have you had your pilot's license?"

"About fifteen years. Does that make you feel any better?"

"Loads," she admitted, and for the first time since seeing him emerge from the hangar, she smiled.

The remainder of the trip passed quickly and pleasantly for L.C. Drex helped her along by patiently answering her questions regarding the numerous gauges and dials on the panel. When he suggested that she might enjoy taking flying lessons, she found she liked the idea. Her feelings about actually working for Drex she would have to sort out later, she decided. For the time being, she thought it best to put his most recent stunt aside and enjoy the afternoon.

The small town where the witness Drex had to interview lived offered little more than a narrow airstrip. L.C. glanced down at the threadlike line of concrete and then back to an unconcerned Drex.

"Frightened?" he asked knowingly.

"Not really." L.C. found to her surprise that she really meant it. She'd been afraid of the smaller plane, she reasoned, but not that Drex couldn't handle it.

The first order of business, once they landed, was to rent a car.

"I really don't think we'll be swamped with indecision," L.C. laughed several minutes later as she walked back over to the dusty counter where Drex was waiting.

"Why not?"

"There are only two vehicles available. One closely resembles my Chevy, and the other one has a flat tire."

"Great," Drex muttered, tapping his fingers impatiently against the counter.

The young, gum-chewing attendant reappeared brandishing two sets of keys. "Take your choice," he said breezily, immediately transferring his undivided attention to L.C.

Beside her, L.C. could feel Drex bristling. "I'd like one that doesn't have a flat tire, something that runs. Do you think that's possible?" he asked sharply, his gaze like black points of steel.

"Sure thing." The unabashed youth grinned at L.C., ignoring the threatening look Drex was giving him. He placed his hands on the edge of the counter and vaulted over like a young colt. "Follow me and we'll see what we can find."

Drex's muttered oath beneath his breath brought a smile of amusement to L.C.'s lips. "I wouldn't antagonize him if I were you," she warned. "We just might find ourselves walking."

"Oh, I doubt that," he said. "That gum-chewing idiot will go to any lengths to find *you* a car."

"Dear me," she chuckled. "Are you jealous that he isn't properly impressed with a big-time lawyer from the city?"

"Not at all. I am jealous as hell, however, of the way he undressed you with his eyes."

"I see."

"You don't see anything," Drex snapped, his long strides almost forcing L.C. to run in order to keep up with him. "I didn't bring you along so that every redneck in the state could ogle you. And in the future, would you please dress with more care? Every move you make in that damn blouse shows the shape of your breasts."

"Dress with more care?" L.C. asked amazed. She quickly looked down at the front of her tailored blouse with disbelief. Each button was closed, it didn't bind in the least, and the sleeves buttoned neatly around her wrist. "I think you're crazy," she whispered as they approached the waiting attendant. He's also jealous, a tiny voice whispered with just a touch of pleasure.

Drex shook his head and muttered something unintelligible as he stared at the only car available. "Is this the best you can do?" he asked sharply.

" 'Fraid so." The young man grinned, not the least perturbed by the sharpness of the question. "It'll get you wherever you're going and back. By the way, where are you going?"

"Out to the Sampson place. Will Sampson's. You know him?"

The young man nodded. "Sure. Will's a good friend of mine." Then without batting an eye he asked, "What do you want to see him about?"

"It's a private matter," Drex retorted. He

109

reached out, opened the passenger door, and all but pushed L.C. into the front seat. While he walked around the car, the attendant leaned down and grinned at L.C. "You work for him?"

"Yes."

"Is he always shootin' off sparks like a hot pepper?"

Hearing Drex referred to as a hot pepper was her undoing. "No. He's usually very nice," she managed to say against the laughter bubbling up in her throat.

The engine roared to life, drowning out whatever else the young man was saying. Drex backed out of the parking slot with such speed, the young man was forced to jump aside to keep from having his foot smashed.

"Really, Drex!" L.C. frowned. "You almost hit him."

"Good. Maybe it'll teach him to keep his eyes and nose where they belong." He fished a folded sheet of paper from his inside jacket pocket and thrust it at L.C. as they roared onto a blacktop road and headed east. "Those are the directions to Sampson's house. How about being my navigator?"

Though she read the directions carefully and got them to the Sampson place without a hitch, part of L.C.'s thoughts were taken over with Drex's little jealous fit back at the airstrip. It was a very interesting revelation, she mused as she walked beside him up the brick walk to the front door. A jealous Drex was almost as comical as the practical joker.

The interview went off without a hitch. Not only did L.C. take down every word in shorthand, she recorded the conversation as an added safeguard—as per Drex's earlier instructions. But even as she listened, with her right hand flying over page after page of the stenographer's pad, she had to admit that Drex Halloran was a master when it came to extracting information. He handled Will Sampson so skillfully, she had no doubt that if the poor man had been in possession of some top secret government information, Drex would have been cognizant of that information within thirty minutes after the interview began.

L.C. wondered what Drex was like in the courtroom. She made a mental note to find out when he would next be trying a case. Seeing him in action would be a rare treat indeed.

The name Albert Linsey began cropping up in the conversation—an eye witness to the accident in which Drex's client was injured. L.C. wondered why he, as well as Will Sampson, wasn't being interviewed. To her way of thinking, two such expert witnesses would carry a lot of weight in a jury trial.

The moment they were in the car and headed back to the airstrip, L.C. brought up the subject of Albert Linsey and offered her opinion that interviewing him could only have positive effects on the case.

"I agree," Drex said with an approving nod. "In fact, he's the next item of business on my list."

L.C. sat back, pleased with how readily he'd agreed with her. "Really?" Now that she'd learned exactly who Drex was and how successful he obviously was, she was slightly in awe of him—from a professional standpoint. Personally, he was still the same conniving, manipulative individual she'd been seeing for the past few weeks.

"Why the surprised expression?" Drex laughed.

"Oh . . . I don't know." L.C. shrugged. "In view of the fact that you're probably famous in your field, I suppose I was shocked that you'd think my suggestion a good one. But"—she tipped her head decisively and grinned—"even law students can come up with some useful ideas."

"Only a fool would refuse to accept or acknowledge an excellent suggestion, honey, regardless of who it comes from. Trying a case is more than just researching and presenting it. A good lawyer always has that little something extra up his sleeve—that added element of surprise for his opponent. The first thing a beginning attorney should do is establish himself as unpredictable. That way he can never be taken for granted by the opposition."

"When do you think you'll be seeing this Albert Linsey?" L.C. asked.

"Soon," Drex said. "Want to come along?"

She nodded. "I'd like that very much."

When they reached the airstrip, the same young man Drex had been so short with accepted the key and the fee for the rental car, his dancing eyes rarely leaving L.C.'s amused face.

Drex hustled her toward the plane before she could say more than two words to her newest admirer. "I don't think anything short of a cannonball in the butt would keep that grinning idiot from staring at you," he muttered beneath his breath, his grip on her upper arm firm.

"He does tend to be rather open with his admiration, doesn't he? But I really don't think he means anything by it," L.C. offered soothingly. "In a town this size, I'm sure a new face just naturally makes him curious."

"Correction, my dear. It was your face that made him act like a young jackass," Drex grumbled as they boarded the plane. "He damn sure wasn't interested in my ugly puss."

L.C. laughed softly and then settled back contentedly, idly watching Drex's capable hands as they darted about the instrument panel. The plane began taxiing forward, and she glanced at her watch, noting that it was almost four o'clock and already starting to get dark. By eight o'clock she would be back in her apartment studying.

113

Conversation was sporadic for the next thirty minutes or so, each seeming content being with the other and lost in his or her own individual thoughts. Suddenly L.C.'s gaze, which had been lazily examining the instrument panel, stopped on the compass, passed over it, and immediately swung back. She stared in disbelief at that very informative object.

"Why are we headed northeast?" she asked guardedly.

Drex turned his head and regarded her innocently. "Didn't you say you wanted to be with me when I interviewed Albert Linsey?"

"Of course I did." L.C. frowned. "But I also remember Will Sampson saying Mr. Linsey lives in east Tennessee."

"That's true." Drex's brows were arched humorously and his eyes were gleaming jets of coal.

L.C. chewed pensively at her lip. "I suppose you've planned this—this kidnapping all along, haven't you?"

"Well," Drex said, rubbing at his neck with one hand, "I did give you an opportunity last night to come on your own."

"Opportunity my foot," L.C. muttered angrily. "Was Leslie in on this little trick?"

"Gee, I can't remember," Drex blandly replied. "Look at the sunset." He gestured toward the west. "Isn't it lovely?"

"Need I tell you what you can do with this trip and the lovely sunset?" L.C. cooed, a

114

brief, saccharine smile touching her attractive mouth.

He clicked his tongue. "There is simply no pleasing you."

"Oh, yes, there is. You can turn this plane around and take me back to New Orleans, Mr. Halloran. This may come as a surprise to you, but I've always considered it my right to decide when and if I want to go on trips with men."

"I think that's the way it should be—except on this occasion, of course."

"Really?" She glared at him. "What, pray tell, makes this sleazy, underhanded proposition any different from countless others I've been 'fortunate' enough to receive since first discovering boys?"

"What's sleazy about wanting to be with someone you care about?" Drex challenged her. When L.C. remained silent, he sighed in frustration.

"I resent being manipulated. Can't you understand that?"

"Not completely. Covert manipulation usually means one person taking advantage of another. I'm not doing that to you, sweetheart. But I think the time has come for you to tell me something about your marriage."

"I don't want to talk about it," L.C. said stubbornly.

Drex reached out and cupped her chin, his fingers pressing against her cheek until she turned and faced him. "You will, sweetheart,

115

you will. I don't mind doing battle with anything or anyone, but fighting the ghost of the bastard who hurt you is pure hell. I want to know it all. What your marriage was like, how he treated you—all of it."

L.C. stared into his eyes, unsure of the dark, flaming emotion she saw there. With Drex it always seemed to be a case of him pushing her, daring her to go one step beyond the boundaries she'd set for herself. But what would happen when—if—she crossed over that last barrier, the one she'd sworn would protect her heart from being broken again?

CHAPTER EIGHT

For the remainder of the flight to Knoxville, L.C. made no effort to break the uneasy silence inside the cockpit of the small plane. After several attempts at conversation, Drex withdrew into his own stony silence, his lips compressed into a tight, straight line of annoyance.

Let him stew, L.C. thought maliciously. He arranged this little adventure, so if it wasn't to his liking, then that was just too bad.

After landing and making arrangements for a rental car, Drex gave L.C. an unsettling glance. "I think the first thing we need to do is some shopping."

"For what?" she asked, avoiding the directness of his gaze as he held open the car door for her.

"Oh," he drawled in an irritating fashion, "just a few minor things, such as a toothbrush for you, along with a change of clothes." He ducked inside the car, his face uncomfortably close to hers. "Do you need pajamas, Laurin? Or what about a sexy nightgown? Better still,

117

do you sleep in the nude? Even though you're diminutive, you have a lovely figure. I can just imagine certain . . . er . . . interesting points playing peekaboo through a shimmering barrier of lace."

L.C. stared straight ahead, her face as red as a beet even as the corners of her mouth twitched suspiciously. She was determined not to laugh. Darn him, he'd carefully orchestrated this entire trip to suit himself, and she wasn't about to let him off the hook that easily.

"I'll take the toothbrush—and toothpaste," she airily replied, and then looked down at the blouse, skirt, and blazer she was wearing. "I suppose I could wear this same outfit tomorrow. But you won't have to worry about spending company money on a gown. I prefer sleeping nude."

"You do?" Drex drew back a fraction and regarded her curiously. "Funny—I'd have thought you'd swathe yourself in yards of flannel at night."

"Really?" She forced herself to meet his dancing eyes. "How about you, Drex? Do you sleep with or without pajamas?"

"Without."

"Good," she said briskly. "Now that that small problem has been taken care of, shall we get started? It's been a long day and I'm tired."

"Certainly," he stated smoothly. Within

118

seconds he was behind the wheel and they were on their way.

After several minutes of driving, L.C. looked questioningly at Drex. "Am I to assume you've made reservations for us for the night?" He seemed to have no difficulty finding his way around the city, and that irked her.

"Did you think I was going to make you sleep in the plane?" he asked cockily.

"At this point, nothing you did would surprise me." She felt the car brake and saw the rapid blinking of the turn signal. "Why are we stopping here?"

"There's a shopping mall over there. See it?"

L.C. nodded, then crossed her arms across her chest, her mouth set in determination. If he thought she was actually going through with his crazy notion of "picking up a few things" for her, then he was in for a big surprise. Nothing short of dynamite would get her out of the car.

Due to the lateness of the hour, parking wasn't a problem. Drex switched off the engine and turned to his less than enthusiastic passenger. "According to my watch we have about forty-five minutes left before the stores close."

"I'll wait for you," L.C. replied coolly.

Drex shrugged, then opened the door and stepped out. But instead of going on without her, he strode around the front of the car and

119

opened her door. Before she could do more than blink her eyes, she felt his strong hands on each of her upper arms and felt her body being lifted from the seat. When her feet touched the pavement, she swung around and glared at him. "I have no desire to go shopping with you."

"Of course you do," he said. "I seriously doubt you want to wear those clothes two days in a row and there's no reason why you should. Since I 'kidnapped' you, it's my place to see that you're provided with whatever you need to be comfortable."

"You could start out by 'providing' me with my own bed," she said as several late shoppers walked past them. "I wouldn't put it past you to have dreamed up this other witness. You probably had that Sampson fellow throw in his name as a decoy."

"You really think I'd do something like that?" Drex asked innocently.

"Yes!" L.C. said unhesitatingly. "In the short period of time I've known you, I've come to the conclusion that you are completely without scruples. I've never known anyone as singleminded or devious as you."

"I'm crushed."

"In a pig's eye!" she retorted. "I should live long enough to see you crushed."

"Now that you've shattered my self-esteem, shall we get on with our shopping?" he asked calmly. As he spoke, his hand slipped beneath her elbow and he began leading her toward an awninged entrance. "We can finish our conversation later over dinner."

"Dinner is out," L.C. flatly announced with as much dignity as she could muster while being hustled inside. "I'll have a hamburger in my room."

"With or without mustard?"

She gave him a sizzling look and opened her mouth to rail at him again, just as an attractive saleswoman approached them. Much to her chagrin, L.C. found herself standing by helplessly while Drex displayed his most potent charm. Then she was whisked to the lingerie department. Rather than stand and argue in front of a total stranger, she reluctantly gave the salesclerk her sizes, painfully aware, every humiliating second, of Drex standing beside her, grinning like an idiot. When she would have snatched the newly purchased articles of clothing and rushed from the store, she heard her tormentor calmly ask to see some nightgowns—preferably in peach.

"Really, I don't—"

"Of course you do, sweetheart," Drex interrupted her, the husky timbre of his voice causing the saleswoman to stare longingly at him, and instilling in L.C. an urgent desire to choke him. "My wife is one of those rare individuals who hates to spend her husband's money," he said affectionately as he slipped an arm around L.C.'s waist and pulled her close to him, his lips touching her forehead.

A sudden gleam replaced the murderous

intent in L.C.'s eyes as she withstood the syrupy show of affection from her "husband." "You're so generous," she murmured sweetly, her words followed by a gentle caress of one slim hand against his steel jaw. She looked at the saleswoman and shrugged. "What can I say? He's such a pussycat. If I don't do as he wishes, he pouts like a little boy." A quick glance to see how Drex was taking her abrupt change made L.C. want to do cartwheels down the aisles of the store.

There was a distinctly mottled color to the dull flush that crept up from his neck to his face. His dancing eyes had turned from vastly amused to darkly suspicious, watching L.C.'s every move like a huge cat stalking a canary. She knew she would pay later for her teasing, but at the moment, outfoxing him at his own game was the highpoint of her day.

After going into feigned raptures over a lovely peach-colored gown and matching peignoir, which Drex bought, L.C. then caught him by the hand and hustled him over to sportswear, where she purchased a skirt and a blouse. She paused beside a tweed blazer, casually lifted the sleeve, then dropped it.

"I think that's all," she said sweetly to an impassive Drex, who had been constantly at her side, carrying her packages and paying for her purchases. Privately, L.C. was screaming inside as she kept a mental tally of all she'd spent. Between Leslie and Drex she would be well and truly broke by the time she payed for these recent shopping forays.

"Are you sure there isn't anything else you'd like to look at?" Drex asked smoothly as they made their way toward the exit.

"Positive," L.C. retorted as visions of bologna sandwiches as a steady diet stretched endlessly in her mind.

When they arrived at the hotel, L.C. was out of the car like a shot.

"In a hurry?" Drex chuckled, one long arm snaking out and opening the heavy front door for her.

"You'd better believe it," she muttered. "Knowing you as I do, I wouldn't be at all surprised to find us sharing a room."

Five minutes later she found herself staring at the desk clerk. "What do you mean, that's the only room you have left?"

"I'm sorry, ma'am," the short, stocky man said, looking quickly from a calm Drex to the visibly upset L.C. "A suite is out of the question." He obviously misunderstood her anger. "The university is having a big alumni party, and there are two conventions starting this evening. You're lucky your husband called when he did. Otherwise, we couldn't have kept even that room for you."

"He is not—"

"There will be no problem with the room, I'm sure," Drex spoke up, then gave a peculiar whoofing sound when the heel of L.C.'s shoe descended on his foot near the ankle. He

123

ripped the key from the desk clerk's hand, grabbed L.C. by the elbow, and rushed toward the bank of elevators. "I hope you're satisfied, Ms. Carlyle," he bit out angrily, once the heavy door swooshed closed behind them and he'd savagely punched the number of their floor. "I think you've broken my damn foot."

L.C. quickly scooted to the farthest corner of the elevator and regarded him icily. "I wonder why that particular statement fails to evoke the slightest bit of sympathy in me?" The insufferable toad, she thought, every fiber of her small being vowing revenge.

"Probably because you're a heartless little bitch," Drex roared at the exact moment the doors opened on their floor and they found themselves facing two astounded matronly ladies.

Drex ignored the pointed scrutiny of his small audience, grabbed L.C. by the arm, and took off down the corridor like a fullback.

"Do you mind?" L.C. maneuvered her hand around the packages she was carrying and tried to pry his fingers from around her arm. "In case you haven't noticed, my legs are considerably shorter than yours, and I refuse to dangle in your wake like an obedient squaw."

Drex abruptly stopped before a door, thrust the key into the lock, and opened it. He looked down at L.C., his fulminating glare removing a rather large portion of her self-confidence. "You'd do well to get that cute little ass of yours inside, Ms. Carlyle, before I do it for you. At the moment you can believe me when I tell you that bringing you along, so far, has been as pleasant as a five-inch thorn in my drawers!"

She flared up. "Need I remind you that it wasn't my idea in the first place?" She took two steps into the room and stopped. Instead of the two double beds she'd been expecting, the room was dominated by a bed big enough to sleep ten people!

"Now what?" Drex threw over his shoulder as he slammed the door. He limped to the bed, where he threw the remaining packages and the suit bag that he'd pulled out without a hint of an apology when they got off the plane. "Am I to assume from your mulish expression that you don't like the room?" He dropped to the edge of the bed, rested his injured foot on his knee, and removed his shoe and sock.

"It's a lovely room," L.C. grudgingly admitted. "It's just unfortunate that I have to share it with such a jackass." She meant to sweep by him with her nose in the air, but the sight of a purplish bruise and small abrasion on the top of his bare foot made her pause, genuinely shocked by the damage she'd done. "Oh, I'm sorry. That must be painful." She'd wanted to inflict pain, she told herself, but she hadn't wanted to draw blood.

"You're damn right it's painful," Drex said

125

in clipped tones. "It hurts like hell. I hope you're satisfied, now that you've crippled me."

L.C. smiled in spite of herself, wondering why she'd bothered wasting a moment's sympathy on the brute. She reached out matter-of-factly and gently touched the bruised area with the tip of one finger. "I seriously doubt you'll be on crutches for more than a week. Since you obviously had time to give more thought and planning to our little trek than I did and brought along your luggage, maybe you have something in your shaving kit that we could put on this."

"You never miss an opportunity, do you?" Drex muttered petulantly, his attention seemingly devoted to his injury.

"If it's sympathy you're looking for, Mr. Halloran, then you're in for a big disappointment," L.C. said bluntly. Without asking further, she walked around him and reached for the suit bag and unzipped it. After finding his shaving kit and opening it, she unearthed a small tube of antiseptic cream she knew from experience would help the cut as well as burn like the very devil. "Have no fear, O brave one," she chortled. With a mean grin she walked over and waved the medicine beneath his nose. "I've found the very thing that will cure you."

"That's never been opened. What is it?" Drex asked suspiciously as he clutched his foot with both hands.

"Medicine for your boo-boo," L.C. said with a perfectly straight face. "And don't look as though I'm offering you hemlock. This came from your very own shaving kit." She sat beside him on the bed and motioned for him to place his foot in her lap.

Like someone facing an executioner, the brave giant beside her—heretofore seemingly unafraid of man or beast—eased his leg hesitantly across her thighs, his dark eyes darting back and forth as though expecting any minute to see her whip out a knife and amputate his foot.

"Are you always this chickenhearted?" she grinned as she uncapped the ointment and applied a generous amount to his foot.

For the first moment or two Drex was quiet under her ministrations, adopting an expression of resigned suffering. But as the cream penetrated the broken surface of the skin, his eyes widened and he gasped as if a sword had been plunged through his chest.

"Dammit to hell!" he exploded, the force of his voice causing L.C. to jump. Drex grabbed his foot and jerked it away from her. "I knew I shouldn't have trusted you!"

"My goodness," she shrugged innocently. "I've never seen a big, strong man carry on so over a moment or two of discomfort."

"Moment or two of discomfort hell," he roared. "My foot feels like you poured gasoline on it and struck a match."

L.C. clicked her tongue as she walked into

127

the bathroom to wash her hands. "Would you like me to call room service and have them send up something for you before I leave?" she called out.

"And just where do you think you're going?" Drex asked from directly behind her.

L.C. gave a startled squeak of surprise and swung around to face him. "Must you sneak up on me that way?" He was leaning against the doorjamb, one arm braced over his head, staring angrily at her. After a moment or two L.C. turned and placed the hand towel on the rack. "Is your foot better?"

"Yes—no thanks to you," Drex said shortly. "Would you like to go out for dinner or would you rather eat here in the room?"

"Out," she said without hesitating. There was no way in the world she was going to sit down to dinner with him in a room with a bed as big as an ocean liner. But what about later? she asked herself, and immediately her thoughts went into a tailspin. Without being aware of doing so, she turned her head and stared at the bathtub, wondering how she was going to be able to convince her new roommate that it would be as comfortable as a feather bed.

"If you're measuring that for me, you can damned well forget it," Drex said, reading her thoughts perfectly. "I'm sleeping in the bed, and so are you." His face was a study of determination, and she didn't like it one little bit.

"You think so, huh?" L.C. went to push by him, only to find herself neatly locked between two strong arms and brought up close to a body as unyielding as granite. "Do you mind?" she demanded loftily, trying to ignore the accelerated beating of her heart and the sudden rush of warmth that was creeping over her. Damn him! She didn't want to be in his arms. He'd tricked her—not once, but several times—and she was still angry.

"I know so, to answer your first question, and yes, to your second one," Drex said huskily as his hands began a slow seductive journey up and down her back, coming to rest on the slight swell of her buttocks and pressing her intimately against his thighs. His lips touched hers lightly, his tongue teasing and tasting the outline of her mouth until L.C. felt herself on fire for him. When his tongue demanded entrance into her mouth, she complied eagerly. Her arms had long since found their way to his shoulders and her fingers were caressing the hair at his neck. They eased around to his face, feeling, exploring, touching like those of a blind person committing his features to memory, then back to his nape, molding themselves to the shape of his neck and shoulders.

She felt his hand at the front of her blouse and eased back in order to give him access, her anger slipping effortlessly from her thoughts. When he cupped one firm breast and let his thumb slowly circle the pulsating nipple, L.C. felt the unwitting spiral of desire coiling within her. She sucked in her stomach and felt her body tighten and tense with excitement. Of its own volition, her body pressed closer to him. A flame arose within her so intense, so magnetic, it held her in its grip with a force far stronger than any she'd ever known.

"Do you still want me to sleep in the bathtub?" he whispered as his lips touched her neck and throat while his hands gently caressed the sides of her breasts, then withdrew and began buttoning her blouse.

A long sigh of unfulfillment escaped L.C. She allowed her forehead to rest against his chest, her senses protesting the withdrawal of his touch, while her mind was telling her that she should be thankful Drex stopped when he did, or they would have ended up on the king-size bed.

"No," L.C. murmured as she slowly raised her head and stared at him. "Not at this precise moment at any rate. But"—she smiled ruefully, raking the knuckles of one small fist gently against his chin—"after I've had dinner and regained my fighting spirit, I'll probably throw you out of the room. What do you think of that?"

Drex grinned. "I think, Ms. Carlyle, that I'll just have to redouble my powers of persuasion. What do you think of that?"

CHAPTER NINE

Since neither Drex nor L.C. was familiar with Knoxville, and since it had been a long and exhausting day, they opted to have dinner in the hotel dining room. Although it occurred to L.C. that, for all the attention she was paying to her surroundings, they could just as easily have been sitting in a tree.

In the privacy of her own thoughts she was attempting to come to grips with the new situation: the sleeping arrangements she'd first decided upon had been ditched, and she would, more likely than not, share the king-size bed with Drex. The more L.C. thought about it, the more it seemed the most logical conclusion to the relationship that had sprung up so effortlessly between them.

But is that what she really wanted? a tiny, cautious voice asked. And L.C. knew it was. From the beginning, that first night at the ball when she'd looked up and found herself staring into Drex's dark eyes, she'd felt a certain inexplicable urge to challenge him.

Challenge indeed, her bruised ego scoffed.

But, L.C. silently argued, she had done just that. Her motives had been born of a quiet desperation, fed by the cruel taunts thrown at her by Charles. Taunts that had stayed with her, and were still a conscious part of her actions and attitudes toward men in general.

Drex broke into the thoughts crowding her head. "Have you got it all straight in your mind now, or do you still need more time?" He was sitting relaxed in his chair, one hand around his drink, the other idly toying with his fork.

"I beg your pardon?" L.C. asked, startled. She hastily raised her wineglass to her lips and took a gulp.

"Have you decided how you're going to seduce me?" he asked in a faintly amused voice.

"What makes you think that?" she hedged, knowing all the while that the expression on her face was a dead giveaway. She tipped her nearly empty glass toward him and smiled, her lips stiff. "May I?"

"Certainly," he said obligingly, leaning forward to refill her glass. He sat back, his gaze pointedly studying her. "You forget, Laurin, that it's my business to know what people are thinking. I've had years of experience judging clients, ascertaining the true meaning behind a supposedly casual remark or action, as well as learning to distinguish between truth and lies. Motivation has always determined the manner in which we handle our lives, and always will."

"Meaning?" She shifted uncomfortably in her chair.

"Meaning the treatment you received from your ex-husband made you more determined than the average woman to prove your sensuality."

"I wasn't aware that you held a degree in psychology as well as law," L.C. remarked curtly. "Do you make a habit of analyzing all the women you meet, or have you decided I'm in need of your expertise more than the others?" She took a sip of wine. He was correct in his assessment, uncannily so. But it was one thing to be aware of certain things about oneself and another to be told those things by someone else—especially someone like Drex Halloran.

"There's no need to get angry," Drex calmly replied. "I have no objection at all to being 'used' by you. In fact," he said huskily, his eyes smoky with desire, "I'm looking forward to it."

L.C. briefly closed her eyes against the compelling invitation she saw in his dark gaze, wishing with all her heart she were miles away from the softly lit room, the small, intimate table, and the one man who seemed more than capable of igniting each of her senses to a point of excruciating passion.

Suddenly she felt the touch of his large hand gently removing her fingers from the stem of the wineglass and then caressing her palm and wrist. "Don't be embarrassed,

Laurin," Drex said quietly. "Do you really think I'd be such a willing victim if the outcome wasn't something I desired just as strongly? I'll admit my reasons are different from yours, but they present just as great a challenge."

L.C. forced herself to look at him then, knowing that the time for pretense was over —if it had ever had a place in their relationship to begin with. "How can you remain so calm when you know my reasons for seeing you? You are right," she boldly admitted. "I know the moment I looked into your eyes that first evening that there was something special about you."

"What did you see, Laurin, when you looked at me?"

"I saw ruthlessness and strength—tempered with a certain gentleness."

"Now who's being the psychologist?" Drex smiled.

She shrugged. "I suppose I am, but I did see those things. And when we danced, I found that being in your arms felt good."

"So you decided that since I wasn't repulsive to you, I'd be the perfect candidate on which to try out your feminine wiles—correct?"

"Something like that," L.C. admitted somewhat ruefully. Now that the subject had been brought out into the open, she was surprised to find it wasn't difficult at all to discuss her initial plan to seduce Drex. Although, she told herself, somewhere in between there had arisen certain feelings for him she wasn't ready to examine too closely.

"There is one thing that fascinates me, though, about the premise upon which you've based your . . . er . . . shall we say experiment?" Drex spoke so smoothly L.C. was sure he was laughing at her.

"What's that?"

"The realism with which you've conducted each phase of our being together." He grinned. "If I didn't know better, I'd swear you've enjoyed being in my arms almost as much as I've enjoyed having you there."

L.C. found the remark amusing even though she knew he was teasing her. "You'll do until someone better comes along," she said over the rim of her wineglass.

"Well, now," Drex drawled lazily, "it looks as though I'll have to see to it that that doesn't happen, won't I?" His gaze touched on her glass, which was again nearly empty. "It also looks as though I'll have to carry you out of here if you keep on drinking that wine like it was water."

"Would that embarrass you?"

"Not in the least. I'd hoist you over my shoulder and pat your cute little behind all the way to the room."

"Has anyone ever told you that, in addition to all the other things I saw in you, you're also crude?" she asked spiritedly.

"No. But then, I've never been singled out

as a guinea pig either. It brings out my caveman instincts."

Their quietly serious mood had given way to lighthearted teasing, but underneath the innocuous remarks that continued while they were eating, L.C. sensed a different tone: there would be nothing funny about the situation when they returned to their room.

"Why don't you order dessert?" Drex suggested when he saw her pushing her food around on her plate, with only an occasional bite going to her mouth.

"No thanks." L.C. shook her head. "I'm really not hungry."

Drex made no comment, wondering if he'd done the right thing by forcing her to come with him. It was a first with him, having to resort to kidnapping—of a sort—in order to be with a woman. But then, he mused, nothing about his relationship with Laurin had been usual. In fact, he told himself, he'd spent more time actively pursuing her than any woman he'd known—and for what? She'd admitted that he was merely an instrument in a not too realistic game she'd concocted to prove herself a desirable woman. And even before she'd actually confirmed his suspicions, he'd known she was still hurting from her marriage to a man totally devoid of feeling.

And yet, Drex thought determinedly as he watched the emotions flickering across L.C.'s face, knowing her motives hadn't deterred him in the least. Why this was so still wasn't clear to him. It had nothing to do with his wanting something as permanent as marriage, did it? Of course not, he hastily decided. He'd been involved in the practice of law too long not to look upon the supposedly blissful state of matrimony with a jaundiced eye. In his work he'd seen sane, normal people turned into scheming, vengeful facsimiles of their former selves, screaming and hurling insults as they tried to destroy the partners they'd promised to cherish and protect. No, he reassured himself, it wasn't marriage he was seeking with Laurin, but a normal relationship with no strings attached. Though as he continued to stare at her, he could not think of a single reason why they couldn't share the rest of their lives together—or certainly a large portion of them.

There was a thoughtful silence pulling at each of them as Drex led L.C. out of the dining room, across the lobby, and into the elevator. Before the doors could close, another man stepped inside and nodded politely, keeping his eyes on L.C. She immediately felt Drex's strong arm behind her, his fingers biting into her waist.

"Sleepy, sweetheart?" he asked huskily, his lips brushing against her forehead.

For a moment L.C. was tempted to stick out her tongue at him. Sleepy indeed! His actions, where other men were concerned, including his bad temper, reminded her of a strutting rooster jealously guarding his flock of hens.

She looked up at him and smiled sweetly. "Not at all, dear. But I think you should have an early night. Remember what the doctor said, you aren't as young as you used to be."

Mercifully, at that moment, they reached their floor. As L.C. flashed her undaunted admirer a beautiful smile, she felt the hand at her waist tighten and found herself being lifted off the floor and hauled from the elevator like a sack of potatoes.

"Really!" she exclaimed from her not too elegant position on Drex's hip. "Don't you think you're acting rather childish?"

"Perhaps," Drex snapped. He didn't stop until he reached their room, when he set her on her feet and fished the key from his pocket. He opened the door and pushed her inside.

L.C. whirled around to face him. "Well at least you're man enough to admit it."

"Man?" he mimicked sarcastically. "I thought your portrayal of me in the elevator as an over-the-hill washout was brilliantly done. I'm sure that grinning jackass ogling you thinks you're a sexy young wife saddled with a middle-aged anemic husband." Drex glared at her, his fists planted on his hips, his feet spread apart.

"My, my, Halloran." L.C. shook her head dispassionately. "When you're on the receiving end, it ceases to be funny, doesn't it?"

"What's that crack suppose to mean?"

"Why, nothing, except that I'm usually the butt of your practical jokes. I've had off-color singing telegrams, I've been nearly roasted in your car, I've been the recipient of enough flowers to enter the Rose Parade, and I've been kidnapped. All the aforementioned little deeds were very capably executed by you. But when I retaliate, you bristle like the overbearing ass you really are."

"Are you finished?" Drex asked angrily.

"For the moment." She removed her blazer and hung it beside the new clothes Drex had bought for her. As her hand brushed against the gown and peignoir, L.C. paused. Unless she wanted to sleep in her half-slip and bra—or in the nude—she had no choice but to don the peach-colored ensemble. Even in that instance Drex had gotten his way, interfering to the point of embarrassment when she'd tried to buy something less flamboyant. She looked over her shoulder at the still furious Drex. "I do hope you'll excuse me while I take a bath. Better still, perhaps you'd like to check it out to make sure there's no strange man hiding in the shower?"

"There's no need," he snapped. "From the full-length mirror on that door"—he nodded toward the dressing room—"I can see into the bathroom. Otherwise, knowing how easily men flock around you, I'd most definitely check it out."

"You're sick." L.C. grabbed the gown from

the hanger and hurried into the bathroom, slamming the door behind her. For the life of her, she fumed as she undressed and began to shower, she couldn't figure out Drex's motives. There were moments, especially where other men were concerned, when he acted like a jealous lover.

While it was flattering to know he was jealous, it left her with a troubled feeling. She wasn't ready to deal with that kind of emotion. All she wanted at the moment was a man who wanted her, someone who would be honest in his feelings, someone with enough sensitivity to be concerned about her feelings of desire and passion. So far, she told herself, Drex had done that. But why did he have to drag other problems in as well? He wasn't some innocent she'd taken advantage of. In fact, she reflected, he'd admitted he was aware of her plans all along; plans she herself had dismissed from time to time.

With a ragged sigh hissing past her wet lips, L.C. reached for the shampoo. She applied it to her hair, her fingers working up a tiny mountain of lather and bubbles. Suddenly a draft of cold air hit her wet, naked body. Unable to open her eyes, she reached out blindly, her fingers pausing when they met a solid wall of warm, hair-covered flesh.

"You are an absolute toad! Get out of my shower immediately!" she exclaimed.

"No can do." Drex caught her fingers, pressed them to his chest, and slowly carried them to his mouth, where he gently kissed each tip. He then placed his large hands on her waist and moved her back, filling the space with his large body.

L.C. tried to turn her back to him, but she slipped and was immediately caught up against a naked warmth from the top of her head to the tip of her toes. "I'm afraid there's no place to run, Ms. Carlyle," Drex murmured silkily, letting his hands slide over the soapy surface of her ribs to the creaminess of her breasts. His thumbs circled the excited hardness of her nipples, creating a throbbing ache in L.C.'s stomach.

After each breast had received his undivided attention, Drex turned L.C. into the shower, his hands quickly washing the last of the shampoo from her hair.

"Now," he rasped huskily, "you'll have to look at me, won't you?"

L.C. opened her eyes, fully intending to eject him from the shower. But when she found herself staring at the planes and curves of his powerful body and thinking how perfect he was, her tongue stuck to the roof of her mouth. Powerful arms and broad shoulders topped a strong, deep chest, generously covered with a thick dark growth of hair. His chest tapered into a trim waist, narrow hips, and long, muscled thighs. The tan she'd so often envied on his face and arms covered his entire body.

"You have a beautiful body." She spoke

slowly, thoughtfully, finally breaking the peculiar silence that had come between them.

"Thank you," Drex said softly, standing perfectly still under her thorough scrutiny.

"Does it bother you when I say you're beautiful?"

"No," he said, "because I know you use the word in its true meaning. If it were someone else, I probably wouldn't appreciate the compliment."

"I should think a man who can accept such a compliment without feeling his masculinity has been insulted is rare."

"I can't answer that," Drex replied solemnly, knowing instinctively that one wrong word from him could send her bolting like a frightened rabbit. "In fact, you're the first person to ever see beauty in the shape and form of my body. I'm thinking you're either a poor judge of what beauty really is or you're incredibly innocent when it comes to men."

L.C. reached out and touched him, letting her fingers slip effortlessly down along his chest to the muscled flatness of his stomach. With a boldness never before tested to such lengths, she let her gaze settle on the most male part of him and then raised her head to meet the dark glow shining in his eyes.

"Are you still angry?" she asked tremulously. Her legs were suddenly as wobbly as her voice, and she felt herself moving toward him.

"I don't think I was ever angry with you,"

Drex said hoarsely as he bent to catch her in his arms and lift her against his chest. "I seem to have a very low boiling point when it comes to you and other men. It makes me want to lock you away so that no one can get to you but me."

"That's not a very healthy attitude, Mr. Halloran."

"I know, Ms. Carlyle, but it's there nevertheless."

Without thinking, L.C. brushed her lips against his waiting ones and closed her eyes against the waves of longing rippling throughout her body. The feel of him—all of him—against her was devastating.

Drex allowed her the playful teasing for a moment, then moved one hand to cradle the back of her head. His mouth moved against hers in an unrestrained, uncontrollable need to consume her. His body was smoldering, and Laurin was the catalyst that could turn the embers to rushing, overpowering flames and bring them to their zenith.

He eased his head back, his breathing harsh and painful. "You do know I'm going to make love to you, don't you?"

"Yes," L.C. whispered.

Drex turned and carried her from the shower, not stopping until he reached the bed, where he laid her down. He remained braced over her, his hands pressing into the mattress on either side of her body, his eyes boring into hers, reminding her of onyx.

"There are some mighty conflicting emotions whizzing around in my head where you're concerned, lady," he said gruffly.

L.C. reached up and cupped her palm along the chiseled line of his jaw, her touch sending a shudder of desire over him. "Don't make this into something other than what it really is, Drex," she softly pleaded. "I've hardly begun to know myself again, and I—"

Her words were abruptly halted when Drex placed a finger against her lips. "Don't say it, Laurin," he muttered harshly as the weight of his body joined hers on the bed. "You will know yourself, and me. Before we're through I'll make you know me as a man—as the *only* man in your life."

Before she could reply, he claimed her lips in a kiss that was almost cruel in its intensity, his tongue running over her teeth, demanding entry to the more sensitive regions of her mouth. L.C. opened herself to him, unable to fight the fingers of desire gripping her, clinging to the only solid thing in the churning world she'd been thrust into—Drex.

Hands and lips became trailing instruments of pleasure, forging relentlessly over each and every part of her body. Her breasts were teased and licked by the tip of his tongue, his lips pulling at the peaks of her nipples. At the same time his fingers were stroking the inner softness of her thighs, caressing her in rapid movements that had her arching her hips in wild, unrestrained greed for total fulfillment.

Each second became a millennium of exquisite torture that made L.C. sure she couldn't bear it, yet knowing she would die if it didn't continue. Her attempt to return to Drex a portion of the pleasure he was giving her was met with a hoarse "Not now, sweetheart. This is your time—my gift to you. We'll have plenty of time later for you to do what you want to me."

He cradled her face between his hands, his breath a warm whisper on her cheeks. "Do you want me as badly as I want you, Laurin?"

"I feel like my head is going to explode, and I'm positive that if you don't take me soon, I'll die. Does that answer your question?"

"Oh, yes, my sweetheart, that answers it so very well." He eased himself into position over her, his arms closing about her like a protective blanket against the beginnings of the storm they'd created. He entered her, and L.C. gave a sharp cry of pleasure that brought a hoarse response from Drex.

"Don't hold back," he encouraged her. "Let yourself go. . . . We'll fly, Laurin Catherine Carlyle, we'll fly to the moon." As he talked, the rhythm of his movements increased, indeed making them fly together. They scaled the heavens, scorching the universe with their passion, then floated to earth still clasped in each other's arms.

The sound of Drex's voice filled L.C.'s ears as she listened to the conversation going on

145

between him and Albert Linsey. Once again she was using the small tape recorder in addition to her notes, and it was a good thing she was; this morning found her mind wandering, filled with scenes from the night spent in Drex's arms.

She glanced up from her pad, her gaze darting over him in quick assessment . . . remembering. It had been early morning before either of them had even thought of sleeping. At first their lovemaking had held a certain urgency, as though each were afraid something would whisk the other away. Later it had settled into a slow but powerful expression of need that blanketed them in a cocoon of sensual pleasure.

When they weren't making love, Drex asked questions about her marriage. At first L.C. refused to discuss her ex-husband. That bitter experience was something she'd only discussed with Leslie. But Drex had been adamant, using the skills of his profession like the expert he was. She had talked, and he had listened. Afterwards he'd held her in his arms, his lips and hands soothing away the unpleasantness, making her forget the heartache and agony she'd suffered.

A tiny flush crept over her face while she stared at Drex, remembering the way their bodies had been entangled when she'd awakened at daybreak. As though sensing her discomfort, he chose that moment to glance up at her. There was a look of quiet command in his eyes, as if admonishing her for daring to be embarrassed by what had happened between them.

L.C. was the first to drop her gaze, unable to deal with his penetrating understanding. She'd accomplished what she'd set out to do—regardless of how faintheartedly—and now knew the total fulfillment of being made love to by a man who was as sensitive to her feelings as his own. She was also confident she'd given him pleasure as well. She had heard it in his voice, felt it in the tremors that racked his powerful body, and that pleased her. And now what happens? a tiny, irritating voice asked.

It was a disturbing question, one L.C. had no answer for. What she did know, however, was that she felt complete, whole again, and Drex was responsible for that. She was content for the moment, basking in the knowledge that all those things Charles had said to her were wrong. A wry grin touched her lips as she stared at the notes she'd taken; it was strange, but she felt like a bird freed from the prison of a cage.

Albert Linsey was a gruff man, cool but cooperative. He was courteous to L.C. but focused his attention on the questions being asked by Drex. This action by their host left Drex in a more cordial mood as he and L.C. drove to the airport.

"From that satisfied expression on your face, I'd say Mr. Linsey's evidence has almost guaranteed a favorable ruling for your client." L.C. smiled.

"Indeed it has. And I'd never have known about him if I hadn't spoken with Will Sampson," Drex said. He took his eyes off the road for a moment, noting the glow in her cheeks. "Have I told you that you look absolutely radiant this morning, Ms. Carlyle? I hope I'm responsible."

"Fishing for compliments, Mr. Halloran?"

"Not usually, but in this particular instance —yes."

"May I ask why?"

For once there wasn't a glib answer from Drex. He looked back at the road while one hand rubbed thoughtfully at his chin. "Would you believe me if I said I don't know why?"

L.C. nodded. "Yes, I would. Believe it or not, your answer pleases me far more than vows of undying love or how you can't live without me. Can *you* understand that?"

"I understand," he said slowly. "But what if I were to tell you that my feelings for you *are* different, that I don't want to lose you? Would that frighten you?"

"Yes."

"I was afraid of that," Drex muttered. "Well, then, my dear Laurin," he continued after several seconds of thoughtful silence, "I'm afraid you're going to have to get used to the idea. You've exploded into my world with a bang, sweetheart, and there's no way I'm going to shake hands with you and calmly walk out of your life."

CHAPTER TEN

The first inkling L.C. had that something was wrong came when she heard Drex swear. She turned her head lazily against the back of the seat and opened her eyes. She'd been half dozing, and was surprised at how quickly she'd gotten over her initial fear of small planes. But then, she told herself, perhaps it had nothing at all to do with planes in general but with the pilot.

"That sounded ominous," she said lazily. "What's happened on such a beautiful morning to make you swear?"

Drex didn't answer, but continued working with the knobs and buttons, muttering beneath his breath.

"Drex?" She spoke his name sharply, coming to an upright position. "Is something wrong?"

"At the moment I'm not sure, sweetheart." He threw her a quick smile meant to be encouraging, but L.C. could sense the tension in his expression. "All of a sudden the damn gauge on the fuel pump has gone haywire."

A multitude of questions rushed to her lips, but L.C. remained silent, gazing at the different gauges on the instrument panel, few of which she understood. "I—is there anything I can do?" she finally ventured just as the engine started to sputter.

Drex didn't bother trying to answer. He was using every ounce of knowledge he possessed to try to correct the situation in which they'd suddenly found themselves. He switched to the auxiliary fuel tank, hoping it would give the engine the extra boost it needed to start up normally again, but it didn't. And in that brief moment of desperation he realized he was experiencing his first high-altitude emergency.

A sudden iciness gripped Drex as he maneuvered the plane into a slow turn, circling to the left in hopes of finding some place for an emergency landing.

"Tighten your seat belt until it hurts you," he instructed L.C. in a quiet voice. He did the same for himself, then began talking to the tower in Knoxville, acquainting them with his problem and the location as best he knew it.

As the plane completed its first three-hundred-and-sixty-degree sweep, Drex spied what looked like the solution to his problem. There was a perfect strip of land nestled between two mountains. He began angling the plane toward that spot, praying it would suffice for an emergency landing.

"Are we going to crash?" L.C. asked. Her

face was pale and her hands were gripping the edge of the seat.

Drex threw her a hasty glance, his heart lurching at the fear he saw reflected in her green eyes. Damn! He was a first-class heel, he told himself scornfully. Her life was in danger and it was all his fault. If he hadn't been so busy thinking about what he wanted and how he felt, she would be at home now. "Hopefully not crash, sweetheart," he said grimly. And at that moment it hit him: her welfare and safety was the most important thing in his life.

He pointed to the narrow strip of land. "I'm hoping to use that as a landing strip. It won't be a soft landing, but I'm praying it will be enough to keep us from crashing." He reached out and touched her face, her skin moist with nervous perspiration. "Listen to me carefully, Laurin. I want you to put your head between your knees and place your arms over your head. Don't move from that position until we've come to a complete stop. Can you remember that?"

L.C. nodded, feeling a peculiar sense of unreality washing over her. She was positive that any second now Drex would look over at her and smile, perhaps crack a joke or even remind her that she was supposed to have dinner with him later in the evening.

But as she turned and looked in front of her, she saw the sides of the mountains on either side of them, as well as the treetops that were becoming larger and larger as the plane lost altitude. And then the most ridiculous thought hit her: they were going to be late for dinner!

"Dammit, put your head down, Laurin!" Drex shouted, reinforcing his demand by placing his hand on the back of her head and pushing with all his might.

L.C. was instantly aware of her face being smashed against her knees and the blood rushing to her head. An eerie silence hovered over them for what seemed like an eternity, but in reality it was only a few seconds. The next thing she was aware of was a peculiar snapping, popping noise and a muffled curse from Drex.

The next few seconds became a nightmare, filled with the sounds of metal being torn apart and glass breaking. L.C. could feel wave after wave of unbelievable jolting against her body as she was held in place by the seatbelt that seemed about to cut her in half. There was a long, shuddering wrench from the plane, then complete silence and calm.

It seemed hours to a dazed L.C. before she could bring herself to move. Her entire body felt as if it had been beaten, and she could feel something wet oozing down her shin. One ankle was throbbing painfully and her left elbow felt as if it had been smashed by a heavy object. Slowly, her movements jerky, she lowered her arms and raised her head. Her glassy gaze saw Drex slumped over the controls. He was unconscious and there was blood trickling from his mouth. About the only thing that kept her from passing out at that moment was the steady beat of the tiny pulse in his throat. He was alive.

She stared trancelike at the sizable limb from one of the many trees dotting the area that had slammed through the left windshield and was now wedged against the back of the seat—where Drex's head had been. From her position she could see that the left wing was nothing more than a mangled piece of metal, barely attached to the plane by a thin support.

"Oh, my God!" exploded past L.C.'s pale, bloodless lips as she stared. She tried to reach out to Drex, but her movements were restricted by the unusually tight seat belt. All thoughts of her own injuries were swept from her mind as she tore the belt loose. She had to get Drex out of the plane, she told herself over and over. Although she had no personal knowledge of planes and crashes, she'd seen enough movies and read enough to know that the possibility of a fire was very real. And with Drex unconscious, he'd have no chance at all.

It seemed a painful, unbelievable eternity to L.C. before she was finally able to drag Drex from the plane to what she considered a safe distance from the wreckage. She dropped down beside his still body, exhausted, her breathing labored. Under normal circumstances she knew it would not have been possible for her to get Drex out of the plane, much less drag his large body the distance she had, but fear had lent her an abnormal burst of strength. Yet even with the evidence plain before her eyes, she was still in a state of shock. This can't be happening, she kept thinking, even as she saw the mangled plane and the unconscious Drex, and as her own injuries began to filter into her consciousness.

With trembling hands she reached into the pocket of her blazer and removed a tissue, pressing it against the ugly scratch on her shin. She caught sight of her right ankle and sucked in a deep breath of surprise. It was twice its normal size, and at the same moment she noticed it, she also became aware of the throbbing pain radiating from it.

A deep groan from Drex brought L.C.'s head swinging around. She saw him try to turn, then gasp in pain and fall back against the ground.

"Drex?" She quickly leaned over him, fear causing her heart to thump crazily. "Drex?" she repeated. "Can you hear me?"

"Laurin?" he mumbled in the barest whisper, his dark head thrashing from side to side. "Don't worry, sweetheart, we'll be all right. All . . ."

L.C. gently placed her hands on either side of his head to still his unconscious movement. "Keep still, Drex," she said quietly, and was surprised when he obeyed her. The blood was

155

still trickling from the corner of his mouth, leaving her with the cold, sobering certainty that he was suffering from internal injuries. She stared at him for several seconds, unconsciously chewing at the corner of her lip. Look in his mouth, she kept telling herself. Look and see if he's cut his lip or his tongue. After several similarly worded commands, her numbed body was able to act.

It was with surprisingly steady hands that she forced open Drex's mouth; she gave a deep sigh of relief at the sight of a deep gash just inside his bottom lip. She turned and looked toward the plane. They would need the first aid kit, blankets, and whatever food there was to be had. L.C. remembered Drex radioing that they were in trouble and giving their position, but she had no idea how long it would be before they would be found.

With every muscle in her body protesting, and her sore ankle flaring painfully with each step, L.C. limped and stumbled back to the wreckage. It took three trips before she assembled the few things she thought were the most necessary items for their survival. After dropping down beside Drex, L.C. glanced up at the outcropping of stone that shielded the spot she'd chosen. It would afford them some protection in case of rain, she decided. In the meantime she would take a quick rest and then try to build a fire. Building a fire was very important when one was lost, wasn't it? She frowned as she managed to cover Drex with a blanket. The awful trembling that had been hitting her body at intervals now took over, and she clasped her arms over her upper body, curling into a fetal position. In seconds she was asleep.

Oh, God, the fire! She had to get up and put more wood on the fire. Without it they would never be rescued and Drex would die. She'd managed to stop the bleeding in his mouth, but he was still talking out of his head, and every time he moved, he groaned with pain.

She must get up, she kept telling herself. But each time she tried, there seemed to be something heavy pressing against her shoulders, something that was keeping her from saving Drex. Drex! She mustn't let him die. She mustn't.

"Drex is all right, honey," a familiar voice assured her. "But if you want to build a damn fire, then that's exactly what we'll do. Of course, we might be asked to leave the hospital, but who the hell cares? Personally, I've never liked the smell of these places."

L.C. struggled to escape the wall of darkness that had held her in its grip for so long, forcing her eyes open. What on earth was Ted doing here? She couldn't remember him being in the plane.

A cool hand touched her forehead, then cupped her cheek. "No, sweetheart, I wasn't in the plane. Drex is okay, and so are you. But it's time for you to wake up, L.C. Come on

157

now, open your eyes and look at your brother's ugly puss. If you don't, my feelings will be hurt."

Ted was all right, L.C. smiled to herself. He wasn't hurt. She did open her eyes then, and found herself staring straight into Ted's dancing green eyes. Eyes exactly the same color as her own. "Wha—what are you doing here?" she croaked, her voice sounding strange even to her.

"I got tired of Central America and decided to spend a few days with you. But when I arrived, I learned you and this Drex character were camping in the Smokies." He leaned down and kissed her on the forehead.

"Camping indeed," L.C. grinned. "I've never been so frightened in my entire life. It was awful."

"I can imagine. However, other than a sprained ankle and a few cuts and bruises, the doctors assure me you're in good shape. You've slept for the better part of a day and a night, but I'm told that was your body's way of taking care of the shock and exposure."

"Is Drex really all right?"

"Acting like a bear with a sore tail, but recovering nicely," Ted chuckled. "He's suffering from a concussion and some broken ribs, and he's making the lives of the nurses miserable. I've stuck my head in his room a couple of times to introduce myself, but on each occasion he was giving somebody holy hell, so I haven't had a chance to talk with him yet."

158

Ted sat on the edge of the bed and looked at L.C. closely. "Is he someone special, squirt?"

"Yes," she admitted. "But at the moment I'm not sure just how special. Things have gone so fast where he's concerned, I feel like I'm on a merry-go-round."

"Then don't rush it," Ted advised, "no matter how hard he pushes. You're young and you have plenty of time."

L.C. squeezed his hand and smiled. "Thanks, Ted. That's the same thing I've been telling myself. Gee, it's good to see you. It's been almost two years since we've had any time together."

"Well, we've got time now. The doctor kept telling me that you could leave as soon as you awakened, providing you were feeling okay. I think you should stay until tomorrow just to be on the safe side."

"What time is it?"

"Early afternoon. You and Drex were brought in yesterday. The fire you kept going enabled the rescue team to find you after only a few hours. You're something of a heroine."

"Some heroine," L.C. said. "I was scared out of my mind. The only thing I could think to do was get Drex out of the plane. I was terrified it would explode."

"Well it didn't," Ted told her, "but it could have. You did the right thing. By the way, I called Mother. She was ready to fly over here, but I assured her everything was under control. She and Clayton want us both to come to

159

Hawaii as soon as you're able to travel. Clever of me, don't you think?"

"Right now it sounds heavenly."

"Speaking of heavenly," Ted said teasingly, "would you like to go visit your friend Drex? I was told that when you awakened, and if you felt like it, you could see him. I think they're hoping your presence will sweeten his personality."

"I'll go," L.C. said, and began fumbling with the sheet and blanket covering her. "I can imagine the trouble he's causing."

Drex's head was bandaged, and beneath the opened pajama top L.C. could see that his chest was also bandaged. One eye was the color of purple grapes, and his bottom lip was twice its normal size. Ted had pushed her wheelchair right up to the bed, and she could feel her chest constrict as she saw how terrible he looked.

"Oh, Ted," she exclaimed. "Are you sure he's all right?" She slowly shook her head. He looked like he was going to die.

"Hell, no, I'm not all right," Drex suddenly snapped, frantically struggling to raise himself up on one elbow. He then turned his full attention to L.C. and Ted. "I've got a bitch of a headache, and my damn chest is throbbing like crazy." He glared menacingly at Ted. "Who the hell are you? I demand that you stop hovering over Laurin and get out of my room."

Ted glanced pityingly down at L.C. "You do

believe in going from one extreme to the other, don't you, kiddo?" Then he looked at Drex. "Frankly, Halloran, I really don't think you're in a position to demand anything." He stepped forward and stuck out his hand. "The name's Ted Bartlett."

"I don't give a damn if you're the Pope," Drex replied, regarding the outstretched hand as if it were a snake. "Get the hell out of this room. I'll see that Laurin is taken care of."

"That won't be necessary," Ted said smoothly, and L.C. could hear the mischief in his voice. "I'm here now, and I'll take care of her."

"The hell you will," Drex bellowed, his face contorted with pain as he tried to maneuver his large body to the side of the bed, then to his feet.

"Ted!" L.C. cried out, but Ted was quicker. He was as tall as Drex, and easily caught the injured man before he could swing his legs over the side of the bed, then eased him back down onto the bed.

"This grinning idiot who has been taunting you, Drex, is my brother," L.C. hastily explained.

"Why the hell don't you have the same last name?" he demanded, his gaze only slightly less hostile than before.

"Because our dear mother believes in the trial-and-error method of picking husbands. L.C. and I are the results of her first two marriages," Ted answered pleasantly.

"Now that that's all settled, Drex, why don't I call your nurse and see if she can give you something that will make you go to sleep?" L.C. asked.

"I don't want to go to sleep," he snapped, reminding her of a small, petulant boy.

"But you have a concussion and broken ribs, Drex," L.C. said. "You have to give your body time to heal."

"I'd much rather have you stay with me," he grinned mischievously as he pushed the edge of his pillow beneath his cheek. "Are you really all right?" he asked. "Everybody kept telling me you were, but in this damn place, getting any kind of information out of anyone is like pulling teeth. How's your ankle?" His large hand reached out and caught L.C.'s, bringing a flush of embarrassment to her face in light of Ted's undisguised interest. "I want you to stay here until you're well," Drex told her.

"I appreciate that, Drex, but Ted said the doctor told him I could go home in the morning," she said softly. The touch of his hand brought back memories of him making love to her, memories that were precious to her.

"Nonsense!" Drex exclaimed. "There's no one to look after you at your place. I want you here."

"I'll be with her," Ted chimed in, taking a seat on the edge of the bed and smiling pleasantly at Drex.

"You're just full of bright ideas, aren't you?"

he said. "I want her here with me, where I can see her."

Ted glanced at L.C. and shrugged as if saying, He's your problem.

"I think it would be best if I went home, Drex. Ted or Leslie will bring me over to see you every day. Besides, it will be a good time to get some studying done."

He didn't like her decision, he decided, but there seemed little he could do about it. He opened his mouth to speak, then stopped and looked pointedly at Ted. "Do you mind stepping out into the hall for a few minutes? I want to kiss your sister, and I'll be damned if I'll let you leer over my shoulder while I do it."

"Christ!" Ted pretended to be shocked. "You look like you're barely able to breathe, and you want to make love to my sister?" He turned to a grinning L.C. "Beware of overbearing men, squirt. They tend to think they own the world and everything in it." He pushed off the bed and regarded them with amusement. "Remember, sweetie, the poor man has been through a lot. Don't let him overtax himself."

Once they were alone, Drex frowned. "Is he always such a busybody?"

"He isn't really," L.C. laughed. "Ted is—" she shrugged. "It's difficult explaining him. But he's a very nice brother, and I love him very much."

Drex inched closer to the side of the bed

and leaned forward, his gaze drinking its fill of her. "Didn't you tell me once that he was a news correspondent?"

"Yes, and he's a very good one," L.C. murmured, feeling the heat revealed in his eyes caressing her body.

"I love you, Laurin Catherine Carlyle," Drex murmured without warning.

Without thinking, L.C. reached out and placed two fingers against his lips. "Don't," she whispered.

"Why not?" Drex asked softly. "What's wrong with those three words?"

"Not a thing, under different circumstances," she pointed out. "You and I have known each other only about two months. Our relationship has been wild and crazy and wonderful. After we made love I felt like a whole woman again."

"But?" Drex regarded her closely.

"But I don't want either of us making wild declarations of love. Forgive me for saying this, but it somehow cheapens what happened between us. I feel as if you're only saying what you think I *want* to hear—as if you're trying to reassure me in some way." At the scowl settling over his face, she rushed on, "Don't get me wrong, Drex." She smiled gently. "It only proves what I've come to know about you. You're a very honorable man —when you're not kidnapping me, that is."

"So where does that leave us? Have you decided to stop seeing me?"

"Not at all," L.C. told him. "But I need time. My feelings for you are very special. I need to be able to sort them out in my own way. Can you understand that?"

A rueful twist caught his lips. "If it's the difference between losing you and keeping you, then don't you think I'd damned well better learn to understand?"

"Spoken like the true bully you are," L.C. chuckled. She edged the chair closer and leaned toward him. "I seem to remember something about a kiss? Have you forgotten?"

"No way, sweetheart," he murmured huskily, his lips already teasing her mouth. "And if that smart-ass brother of yours pokes his head in the door, I'll kill him."

CHAPTER ELEVEN

L.C. placed her hand over the mouthpiece and grinned at Ted. "Mother's on a roll today, listen to her." She held the receiver away from her ear so that her brother could listen as well.

"So I really can't understand for the life of me why my two children can't come visit me. I want you, and so does Clayton. You and Ted would love this place, L.C. There's a lovely swimming pool, and the beach borders one side of the estate. Clayton has promised me that if the two of you don't come over, we'll come to you."

"I'm sure Ted and I can manage something, Mother," L.C. said quickly. The thought of having to entertain their energetic mother for any length of time was mind-boggling.

"Tell her we'll come," Ted whispered, wholeheartedly sharing his sister's opinion. They both loved Monica; she possessed the energy of ten people and could easily out-shop, outtalk, and outmaneuver her children.

When she'd married Clayton, they'd both drawn a deep sigh of relief.

"Don't worry, Mother, we're coming," L.C. said, breaking into another running monologue. "It's been over a week since the accident, and the doctor is pleased with my progress. I mentioned I might be going to Hawaii, and he thinks it would be good for me."

Another fifteen minutes went by before L.C. was able to cradle the receiver. She flopped back against the sofa and closed her eyes. "Have you ever considered that we were adopted?"

"I might have been, squirt, but I was with her the entire nine months she carried you," Ted said. "And regardless of bad breaks dealt her in the game of love and marriage, she never once forgot about us."

"No"—L.C. slowly shook her head—"she didn't. She's the top. And in spite of all the disappointments, I really do think she's found it this time. Clayton seems to love her very much."

"He's a nice guy. I like him." Ted picked up a small throw pillow and began tossing it in the air. "So what about Drex? What does he think about your little jaunt to the islands?"

"I really can't say," L.C. replied innocently.

"Hmm. That means you haven't gotten up the nerve to tell him, doesn't it?"

"How well you know me."

"Want me to do your dirty work for you?"

"No. I'll take care of it. I'm sure he'll think

167

it's a splendid idea. But I don't plan on mentioning it for a few days, so don't you dare spill the beans."

Later in the afternoon, as L.C. was dressing to go to the hospital to see Drex, she heard the doorbell. On her way to answer, she was hoping whoever it was wouldn't stay long. Drex would immediately jump to the wrong conclusion if she were late.

She opened the door, her expression running from outright incredulity to concern at the haggard individual leaning against the doorjamb. "Drex! What on earth are you doing out of the hospital?" She reached out and caught his arm to help him inside. His face was drawn with fatigue, and he was pale beneath his tan. "Does the hospital know you've left?" L.C. fussed as she led him over to the sofa.

Instead of meekly sitting down as she thought he would, Drex caught her in his arms and pulled her against him. "God!" he murmured against her hair. "I've missed holding you more than anything."

L.C. pulled back enough to look up at him, exasperation and affection warring for prominence in her face. "You haven't missed it too much," she said sternly. "I've been to see you every day." But when his mouth claimed hers, she promptly forgot the argument and very willingly complied with the inquisitive plundering of his tongue and the unbeliev-

168

ably satisfying sensations created by his hands running up and down her back.

When at last he lifted his head and looked into her eyes, L.C. knew that arguing wasn't going to accomplish a thing. "You look tired," she said softly. "Here, sit down. Would you like some coffee or tea?"

"You're sounding suspiciously like that starched harridan I left at the hospital." He frowned. "I'd like a Scotch and water. I'll also do as you suggest and sit on the sofa. My damn legs feel like jelly."

"You'll get coffee or tea," L.C. said firmly as he pulled her down onto his lap. "Have you forgotten you're still taking medication?"

"I didn't come over to discuss my medical problems," he countered gruffly. He tucked her head in the curve of his shoulder, his arms wrapped securely about her. "I wanted to see you."

"If you'd waited another thirty minutes, I'd have been with you."

He smiled. "I wondered why you were dressed up this time of the day. Where else were you going?"

"Nowhere. I worked this morning and planned on spending the afternoon with you. Any more questions?" She grinned.

"It's too soon for you to be going back to work. Besides, the firm has assumed full responsibility for your medical bills and your salary for six weeks."

"Payment of my medical bills I'll accept, as

well as the salary, until the doctor releases me, which is next week. I couldn't accept anything more."

"Ahh . . . that leads me to another question. Why did you resign from the firm? Does it have anything to do with the fact that I'm your boss?"

"Yes it does," L.C. answered bluntly. "On more than one occasion you've gone to great pains to . . . convey that our relationship is more personal than platonic. I have no intention of being the subject of office gossip. There are other jobs."

"Our relationship has never been platonic," Drex scowled. "Even before we made love the electricity between us was staggering."

"True," L.C. ruefully admitted. "But that still doesn't mean I want you camping in the typing pool. And you would, you know."

"If I give you my word to be the model of decorum during working hours, will you reconsider? If it will make you happy, when we pass in the halls I'll even pretend I don't know you. How's that?"

"Ridiculous, and you know it. You can speak to me, you idiot, but I will not have you barging in and demanding we go for long lunches or making a florist's shop out of the typing pool. It would put me in a very uncomfortable position." She laughed as she evaded the potent weapon of his lips.

"But you saved my life," Drex murmured,

nuzzling her neck and nibbling on her ear. "My associates are grateful and so am I. Why shouldn't I show my appreciation to you?"

"Appreciation is the furthest thing from your mind, and you know it, you fink."

"Not so. Not so at all," he said soberly. "Your thoughtfulness in keeping the fire going and keeping me warm saved me a great deal of pain and suffering."

"You're incorrigible." L.C. sighed and then welcomed his kiss. It left them both breathing unsteadily. "You shouldn't be out of bed," she whispered when she could speak again.

"Don't worry," Drex assured her. "My doctor released me. I'm to take it easy for the next few days and avoid lifting anything heavy. And I shouldn't be upset." He pressed his hand along her hip, holding her tight against his thighs. "But you are definitely upsetting me, Ms. Carlyle. Aren't you ashamed of yourself?"

L.C. smiled lazily into his eyes, feeling his arousal but not in the least regretful. "Not at all, Mr. Halloran." However, she did ease off his lap to sit beside him. "Who's going to look after you while you're recuperating?"

"You."

"Have you forgotten that I'm a law student as well as a working woman?"

"How can I, when you remind me every thirty minutes or so? But even law students and working women have some free time. You could come over to my place and do your

171

studying. You could even pack a bag and spend a few nights with me. I'm sure having you nurse me would speed my recovery."

"Is sex all you think about?"

"With you, yes," Drex easily replied, his gaze holding hers. "Haven't you figured out by now that I want something more than an affair with you, Laurin? I'm thirty-eight years old. When a man my age makes his intentions known to a woman, she can be fairly certain he's serious."

"On the other hand, Drex, when a man has reached your age without making his intentions known to a woman, those same intentions can be construed as unreliable."

"You'll make a damn good lawyer," he said resignedly. "Your argument has merit, I'll agree. But why not give me a chance to prove that you're special? And even though you don't want to hear it, I do love you. I've never told a woman that before." He grinned outrageously. "Doesn't that impress you?"

"No. It makes me realize that you're as gun-shy as I am. You said you've never wanted a lasting relationship with a woman. Well, I wanted one with a man and I thought I had it. I need not recount the story again."

"I resent being even remotely compared with Charles," Drex said harshly. "You know what it can be like with us, and if I have to kidnap you again to make you admit it, then I will."

His stubbornness became more and more

evident as the days went by. L.C.'s hectic schedule before she met Drex was a holiday compared to the pace she now found herself keeping. What with classes, work at the detective agency, squeezing in time to be with Ted, and the time she spent with Drex, she was fast becoming a nervous wreck. Then, too, their relationship was getting more complicated. Her feelings for Drex were such that she couldn't walk away from him without its leaving deep scars. She was being forced to accept that she loved him. Yet, she kept telling herself, she didn't think it unreasonable of her to want to be sure. Hadn't she found love once before and found it gone within a year?

"This has got to stop," she grumbled one Friday afternoon as she hurried home from class, showered and changed clothes, and headed for Drex's apartment. On her way she stopped at the supermarket and picked up steaks for dinner. Drex was recovering nicely, much to L.C.'s relief. Except for an occasional headache, which the doctor had said wasn't uncommon, and some soreness in his chest, he was almost his old self again. He'd been warned against returning to his full schedule for another week, however, due to his work habits and the tremendous amount of pressure connected with each case.

The moment the key he'd given L.C. touched the lock, the door was flung open. "You're late," he said, frowning. He took the bag of groceries, caught her arm with his free hand, pulled her inside, and kissed her—all in one quick motion. Before releasing her, he looked long and hard at her face. "This pace you're determined to keep is killing you. You look exhausted."

"Thanks," L.C. snapped. "That's just what I need to hear." She immediately apologized. "I'm sorry. We had a test today, and I don't think I did too well."

Drex took the groceries to the kitchen, then returned to the living room with a glass of chilled wine for her in one hand, a drink for himself in the other. "Sit," he said.

L.C., who had been standing at the window, smiled at his gruff tone and sat down.

"Mmm," she murmured after settling back against the sofa and taking the first sip of wine. "This is nice." She eased her feet from her shoes and propped them on the coffee table. "I could easily become accustomed to such treatment, Mr. Halloran."

Drex, who had sat down beside her, regarded her seriously. "Why do you insist on pushing yourself so hard? After seeing you and Ted together, I've come to the conclusion that he'd help you if you asked. And from what you've told me about your mother and Clayton, it appears they would as well. There's nothing wrong with accepting help, Laurin. I'm sure they'd accept repayment, if that's what you wanted."

"You're correct on all three points, Drex," she thoughtfully replied as she stared into space. "Looking back, I can see that I wanted to prove something to myself as well as my family. My other motive wasn't as honorable, I'm afraid. Working and studying kept my mind off the unpleasantness associated with my marriage. I suppose Ted and I both get our determination from Mother. If you ever meet her, you'll see what I'm talking about."

"When, Laurin, not if. I'll meet your mother and any other family you have," he replied. "I think it would be nice for her to get to know her son-in-law before the wedding, don't you?"

L.C. stared at him, her expression wary. "I wasn't aware our relationship had been upgraded to engagement status."

"As far as I'm concerned it has," Drex said evenly. "Do you have problems with the idea?"

"A few."

"Such as?"

"Such as the length of time we've known each other and the fact that you're always making plans that involve me without consulting me. There's also a great deal of apprehension on my part where marriage is concerned—fear of failing again is frightening."

"But you do love me?"

"Yes," L.C. said slowly. "I think what I feel for you is love."

"Well, at least that's a step in the right direction." He smiled. "Everything else will fall into place in time."

"You sound very confident."

"I am." Though he didn't bat an eye, Drex was lying. He was terrified of losing her. "Knowing the type of person you are is responsible for that confidence. You would never have told me you loved me if you didn't. So"—he lifted one hand in a gesture of compromise—"if getting you to marry me means changing some of my ways, then I'll do it." He reached out and touched his fingers to her cheek. "I want a marriage for keeps, sweetheart, but mainly I want you, anyway I can get you."

A rush of indecision swept over L.C. as she stared at him. If they'd known each other longer would she be so hesitant? He'd just said he wanted to marry her, that he loved her. Wasn't that enough?

"Ted and I are flying to Hawaii next week." Coward, a tiny voice mocked her. She wanted him, but was too scared to take the risk.

"When was this decided?" Drex asked, his gaze narrowing as he adjusted to this new development. The idea of Laurin being any farther away than her apartment was enough to make him panic. He didn't want her to have time enough to convince herself that they couldn't be happy together, which was exactly what he was afraid she would do if left to her own devices.

"When Mother called a few days ago and informed me she would come to New Orleans if I couldn't see my way clear to visit her."

A ghost of a smile touched Drex's lips. "Is she that formidable?"

"Not formidable." L.C. grinned. "She's an arranger—from people to closets to furniture. I honestly believe that's one of the reasons Ted won't settle down. He's afraid of Mother's visits."

"She sounds like a woman after my own heart." Drex allowed his head to drop back against the sofa, his thoughts racing. Perhaps it wouldn't be a bad idea to place a telephone call to his future mother-in-law. He'd wait, though, until Laurin was on the plane headed for Hawaii. That would give him the perfect excuse. Suddenly he rose to his feet and extended his hand to L.C. "Care to join me in the kitchen while I cook dinner?"

"If you're feeling well enough to cook, why did you sound so awful when you called me today?" She tried to sound stern as she placed her hand in his and was pulled to her feet.

"Because knowing what a softie you are, I knew you'd rush over as soon as you got out of class," he unashamedly admitted. "Smart move on my part, don't you think?"

"I think you're a conniving rat." L.C. sighed as she was towed to the kitchen.

Dinner was delicious. Afterwards, when Drex suggested they move back to the living room, L.C. looked pointedly at the dirty dishes. "Leave them. Betty will take care of everything in the morning."

"Poor Betty. Just who is this Betty?" The tone of her voice betrayed a surge of jealousy.

Drex laughed and caught her close in his arms. "Betty is the woman who cleans for me. She's been spending some time with her daughter, but I got a call from her yesterday, and she starts back in the morning. Okay?"

"That depends. Is Betty over fifty?"

"She is, and her hair is gray as well. Were you jealous?"

"Insanely so." L.C. tapped him sharply on the chin. "I'll not have you entertaining the Bettys of the world behind my back, Mr. Halloran."

"Believe me, Ms. Carlyle, entertaining another woman is the farthest thing from my mind."

"Good. Just so long as you know your place." She held out one slim hand in readiness for his arm. "Shall we retire to the sofa in the living room?" she inquired in a ridiculously nasal twange.

"Certainly, madam," Drex said, joining in the game. Without thinking, he slapped his arm across his torso in preparation for bowing, but let out a howl of pain instead when his still healing ribs protested.

L.C. knew it must have hurt like hell, but to her dismay she laughed until tears came to her eyes.

"I'll have you know, madam, it is not the least bit funny," her now scowling knight said accusingly.

"I know, I know," she agreed between hoots of laughter. "It's not funny at all." She caught his arm and pushed him along. "Men are such children when it comes to a little pain."

"Little pain hell." Drex glared at her as he dropped to the sofa. "I'll have you know I'm recovering from several cracked ribs."

"That is true," L.C. agreed with a suspiciously straight face.

"If I were dying would you show a tad more remorse?"

"Believe me, I'd try."

Drex reached over and dragged her across his thighs. "You're an impudent wench and there isn't an ounce of sympathy in you." His hands began to slowly ease their way over her body, arousing the fires of desire as they touched and soothed. "Stay with me tonight?" he whispered huskily.

"Are you sure you're up to it?" L.C. teased. They both knew she would stay; she'd done so several times since his release from the hospital. But strangely enough, on this one particular subject he never pushed.

Suddenly Drex tipped her off his lap, rose like a sleek cat to his feet, and reached for her hand. "Shall we continue this interesting subject in my bedroom?"

Several minutes later L.C. was lying naked on Drex's king-size bed, her gaze touching lazily, possessively, on each part of his body as he prepared to join her. It was strange, she

179

mused, but for the first time she felt perfectly at ease with her relationship with Drex. Usually there was a lingering shadow of uneasiness—which she was at a loss to understand. Yet tonight there was nothing in her thoughts but a sense of expectancy that she knew would be turned into a glorious completeness after they'd made love.

Drex joined her, pulling her body against the long, vibrant length of him. Then his hands cradled her face. "I can't quite figure out that expression you're wearing," he said huskily.

L.C. smiled and arched her hips intimately against his, anxious for the moment when he would fill her. "That's good. You aren't suppose to know all of my thoughts." She closed her eyes when the now familiar touch of his hands began their incredibly erotic exploration of her body, unable to believe the indescribable pleasure he always gave her.

Moments became intense heartbeats of desire, building and circling upward toward the final climactic moment when they would reach the peaks of fulfillment together. When Drex was confident the journey should begin, he slid into place over L.C., encircling her with his arms and carrying her toward the blinding brilliance of the summit beckoning them.

"It's so lovely here, Mother," L.C. said lazily as she reclined on a redwood lounger beside the sparkling blue swimming pool. She was wearing a bright red bikini, and from the four days she'd been in Hawaii, her skin was tanned a light golden brown. "You seem to have finally found happiness. I'm so glad."

"Clayton is a remarkable man," Monica told her daughter. "He's considerate, gentle, generous to a fault." She spread her hands. "I'm sure I sound ridiculous, but he's all those things and more."

"You aren't ridiculous at all," L.C. replied with a smile. "You sound like a woman who loves her man. That's wonderful."

"But what about you, honey? I've heard Drex Halloran's name several times since you and Ted got here. Is he someone special in your life?"

"Oh, yes," L.C. said. "He's someone special all right." She was silent for a moment, not quite sure how to describe Drex. "He . . . he makes things happen. Do you know what I mean?" She looked helplessly at her mother. "He's also very possessive and jealous, but he's unbelievably gentle with me." She shook her head. "Describing Drex isn't easy. At first there seemed to be so many layers to his personality. When I finally got to the last one, I found I wasn't disappointed. Does that make any sense?"

Monica nodded. "Indeed it does. Sometimes, after all that work, you find you were better off not knowing what was really underneath. When will I get to meet Drex?"

181

"I'm not sure." L.C. hesitated. "He's asked me to marry him."

"And?"

"I can't deny I'm considering it. I love him very much. It's just that entering into something as serious as marriage makes me nervous. It's not one person involved, but two. If it fails, both are hurt. Being responsible for another person's happiness is still causing me some problems. I don't want to be disappointed, and I don't want to disappoint him."

"I'm afraid what you're looking for, honey, is a perfect relationship," Monica said quietly, "and that isn't life. You were so hurt by Charles, you've gone overboard in thinking every area has to be made perfect before the marriage. Good marriages are made over the years by various methods. What works for one can be disastrous for another."

"But how can you be sure?"

"You can't. It's a gamble. And if you make the right choice, then life can have some very rewarding moments. But you can become so exacting that no man will ever be able to please you," Monica said. "That would be a shame, for I'd love to have grandchildren. So far, you and Ted have not exactly outdone yourselves to make my dream come true."

Monica stood and ran a smoothing hand over the putty-colored skirt she was wearing with a cream top. "Are you sure you won't come with us? Clayton is hoping to entice Ted into coming to work for him."

L.C. had to grin at her mother's honesty. "I have every confidence in your powers of persuasion, Mother. Besides, I want to stay here for a while longer. When I go back to New Orleans, I want to be as brown as a berry."

Monica gave in easily enough. "Very well. There's plenty to eat in the fridge. We'll probably be home around ten o'clock."

"Why so late?"

"We thought we'd have dinner at the club."

Later, after she heard the car leave, L.C. turned onto her stomach, the sun leaving her lazy and contented—with one exception. She missed Drex like crazy. Since her arrival in Hawaii four days ago, she'd only heard from him once. And though she'd made him promise not to call her every day, it still irked her that he hadn't done so. Which made her sound like a nut, she told herself as her lids became droopy and sleep overtook her. The last thought before she slept was that if he didn't call her later in the evening, she was going to call him.

There was a feeling of someone stroking her back that reminded her remarkably of Drex, L.C. thought dreamily. But Drex was in New Orleans or Houston, she told herself. She lifted her head slightly, then let it drop back down. Drex should be here with her. Every time she tried to sleep, she dreamed of him. Which, she hastened to remind herself, wasn't at all distasteful. In her dreams they laughed, they talked, and they made love. But

183

when she would awaken and find that it *was* only a dream, there was the taste of disappointment.

That wonderful feeling came again, a strong hand easing down her spine and cupping the fleshy part of her buttocks. "Mmm," she murmured, unconsciously wiggling her bottom against the palm.

"Do you always carry on this way?"

L.C.'s eyes popped open like two champagne corks.

Drex! His face was only inches from hers, the frown on his face at odds with the feeling of warmth that had stolen over her body at his touch.

"What are you doing here?" she finally asked, then pushed herself up and swung her legs around, unintentionally placing herself between Drex's thighs, which closed around her without the slightest hesitation.

"I missed you," he said gruffly, his eyes skimming over the brevity of her bikini. He reached out and let one forefinger trace the line of the tie bra. "I do hope you've kept this little number for the privacy of the pool here, and not the beach."

L.C., almost recovered from the surprise of waking and finding him bending over her, smiled. "Is that all you're concerned with, Drex Halloran? Whether or not I wear a bikini to the beach?"

"It'll do for starters," he said easily, the teasing light in his dark eyes growing stronger.

"There's a hell of a lot of you not covered by those two strips of cloth, sweetheart. In the future, I think I'll help you choose your swimsuits."

"If you don't kiss me within three seconds, I'll strip and parade naked along the beach."

"Oh, well, in that case . . ."

Before L.C. could blink an eye, she found herself flat on her back with the weight of Drex's body pressing her deep into the thick cushion. His lips sought hers hungrily, the four days without her adding an urgency to his need.

"God! I've missed you so much," he whispered as his lips rained a shower of kisses over her face, her neck, and the tops of her breasts.

"If you keep that up you're going to have one frantic lady on your hands," L.C. whispered shakily, "and the poolside is not the best place to make love."

Drex made one final rake with his chin along the V between her breasts, then pushed himself up to sit on the edge of the lounge. His breathing wasn't quite steady, and there was the slightest edge of irritation in his expression. "I'm not sure I like this hold you have over me, Laurin. I feel henpecked," he informed her.

He seemed so dejected she had to laugh. "Will it help if I promise not to tell a living soul?"

"The only thing that will help, Ms. Carlyle, will be for you to marry me."

"Are you sure?"

"Positive."

"In that case, Mr. Halloran, you can consider yourself engaged. These four days haven't been a picnic for me."

Drex gripped her by the shoulders, his expression guarded. "I sure as hell hope you mean what you just said, sweetheart, because I don't intend letting you back out now."

"I mean it, Drex," L.C. said, so softly he could barely hear her. "I'm still afraid, but I'm miserable without you. My mother told me to gamble. So"—she stared at him, the overflowing love she felt for this man showing in her eyes—"I'm doing what my mother told me."

"Good for your mother. Now . . ." He slipped an arm beneath her knees and another behind her shoulders, then stood with her in his arms.

"Drex!" L.C. exclaimed, concern in her voice. "You shouldn't be lifting me. Have you forgotten your ribs?"

He gently lowered her to the concrete apron, a sheepish grin on his face. "I did, but my ribs have an excellent way of refreshing my memory. So much for the macho act." He extended his elbow to her. "Ms. Carlyle," he murmured.

"Mr. Halloran." L.C. tipped her head and smiled as she placed her fingers on his arm.

"May I have the pleasure of your company while I change my clothes?"

"Here?"

"But of course. When I spoke with your mother yesterday, she kindly asked me to stay here during the time it took me to convince her stubborn daughter to become my wife."

"Well, since her stubborn daughter has agreed to become your wife—which she'll probably regret—you can now move to a hotel."

"Oh, no! I still have things to discuss with my fiancée. Such as giving her the lovely engagement ring I brought with me and asking her what I should wear for dinner at the club with her parents and brother."

"You may go nude to dinner, it would serve my mother right. As for the ring, I'm dying to see it. I hope it's huge and splashy."

"It's positively vulgar," Drex replied with a laugh. He pulled her into his arms and held her tight. "I'm so happy, Laurin Catherine Carlyle," he said hoarsely against her hair. "I love you with all my heart."

L.C. eased back so that she could look into his eyes. "No more than I love you, Drex. I'm so glad you came to Hawaii."

"I'd have followed you into hell and back," he told her, with such meaning in his voice that L.C. felt the rush of tears in her eyes. "You're my present and my future, sweetheart." He turned her around then and slipped an arm around her waist. "Your bedroom or mine?"

She smiled. "We'll flip a coin. That way, you won't feel henpecked, okay?"

187

Now you can reserve March's Candlelights *before* they're published!

♥ You'll have copies set aside for *you*
the instant they come off press.
♥ You'll save yourself precious shopping
time by arranging for *home delivery.*
♥ You'll feel proud and efficient about
organizing a system that *guarantees* delivery.
♥ You'll avoid the disappointment of not
finding *every* title you want and need.

ECSTASY SUPREMES $2.75 each

☐ **113 NIGHT STRIKER,** A. Lorin 16391-9-12
☐ **114 THE WORLD IN HIS ARMS,** J. Brandon 19767-8-12
☐ **115 RISKING IT ALL,** C. Murray 17446-5-23
☐ **116 A VERY SPECIAL LOVER,** E. Elliott 19315-X-27

ECSTASY ROMANCES $2.25 each

☐ **410 SWEET-TIME LOVIN',** B. Cameron 18419-3-24
☐ **411 SING SOFTLY TO ME,** D. Phillips 17865-7-33
☐ **412 ALL A MAN COULD WANT,** L.R. Wisdom 10179-4-39
☐ **413 SOMETHING WILD AND FREE,** H. Conrad . . 18134-8-10
☐ **414 TO THE HIGHEST BIDDER,** N. Beach 18707-9-33
☐ **415 HANDS OFF THE LADY,** E. Randolph 13427-7-17
☐ **416 WITH EVERY KISS,** S. Paulos 19744-9-28
☐ **417 DREAM MAKER,** D.K. Vitek 12155-8-17

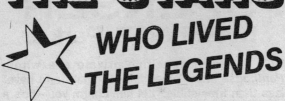

MEET THE STARS

WHO LIVED THE LEGENDS

All-new

Candlelight Newsletter

An exceptional, *free* offer awaits readers of Dell's incomparable Candlelight Ecstasy and Supreme Romances.

Subscribe to our all-new CANDLELIGHT NEWSLETTER and you will receive—at absolutely no cost to you—exciting, exclusive information about today's finest romance novels and novelists. You'll be part of a select group to receive sneak previews of upcoming Candlelight Romances, well in advance of publication.

You'll also go behind the scenes to "meet" our Ecstasy and Supreme authors, learning firsthand where they get their ideas and how they made it to the top. News of author appearances and events will be detailed, as well. And contributions from the Candlelight editor will give you the inside scoop on how she makes her decisions about what to publish—and how *you* can try your hand at writing an Ecstasy or Supreme.

You'll find all this and more in Dell's CANDLELIGHT NEWSLETTER. And best of all, *it costs you nothing*. That's right! It's Dell's way of thanking our loyal Candlelight readers and of adding another dimension to your reading enjoyment.

Just fill out the coupon below, return it to us, and look forward to receiving the first of many CANDLELIGHT NEWSLETTERS—overflowing with the kind of excitement that only enhances our romances!